A DEAD MAN AND DOGGIE DELIGHTS

ALEKSA BAXTER

ISBN: 9781730973871

CHAPTER ONE

I HADN'T BEEN IN THE BAKER VALLEY A DAY BEFORE THE trouble began.

Fancy—that's my three-year-old Newfoundland, full name Miss Fancypants—and I were sitting out back in the yard at my grandpa's reading a book and minding our own business, enjoying the early spring day.

Well, I was reading. Fancy was curled up nearby, her head on her paws, watching the world go by. Not that there was much of a world to see. My grandpa's place is on the edge of town and backs up to a mountainside covered in tall evergreens and aspen trees, so all she really had to see was five hundred feet of trees followed by an incredibly blue sky without a cloud in sight.

Man, I love Colorado.

Anyway. There we were, minding our own business, not bothering a soul, when Fancy jumped up and raced to the fence, barking like a mad woman. And it wasn't her "Hey, is that a dog, can we play?" bark either. It was her, "There's a jerk too close to my home" bark.

I reluctantly set my book aside—I'd just gotten to the good part, too—and dragged myself over to see what was bothering her. She'll usually stop if I just check out whatever it is and tell her she's been a good girl, but as I was walking across the yard I heard someone barking back at her.

That's right. Some jerk on the other side of the fence was *barking* at my dog. Seriously? I mean, what the…? Who does that?

I'd just spent five years living in Washington, DC and not once had someone barked at my dog. They'd stepped away from her like she had the plague, and there'd been an inordinate number of people who thought leaving chicken bones on the sidewalk was just fine and dandy, but none of them had *barked* at my dog.

And, because I was still in big city mode and not "love thy neighbor because you live in a town of a hundred where everyone knows everyone" mode, I stepped up on that little board along the bottom of the fence and told the guy off.

You know what he did? You know what that jerk did then?

He barked at me, too!

He lunged at me like he was going to attack me and barked. Three times. Woof, woof, woof.

I just stared at him like he was crazy. I mean, I'd moved to Baker Valley because it was supposed to be peaceful and nice and this is what I got on my first full day there? Some weird man barking at me? I didn't even know what to do at that point.

Unfortunately, while I was busy trying to figure out if

werewolves might actually be real, which would at least explain the man's ridiculous behavior, my grandpa got involved.

With a shotgun.

There I was, hanging onto the fence, Fancy barking her head off at my feet, and my grandpa comes walking around the side of the house to confront the guy, shotgun in hand. At least I was pretty sure it was a shotgun, I'm not a gun person myself, but it had two long barrels that he pointed right at the guy. *After* cocking it or whatever it is you do with a shotgun to let someone know that when you pull that trigger it's gonna hurt.

"Son, you'd best get on your way." He planted his feet and pointed the gun right at the man, steady as steady could be.

I held my breath wondering if the man was stupid enough to bark at him, too. I figured it was a fifty-fifty chance and I really didn't know what my grandpa would do at that point, but I was pretty sure I didn't want to find out.

Fortunately, the guy just backed away, hands up. "Sorry, Mr. Carver. Didn't mean any offense. Just walking by."

"Well walk a little faster." My grandpa followed him with the gun, eyes flinty and jaw clenched tight. "And next time you leave my granddaughter alone or I'll put you in the ground where you belong, you hear me?"

"Grandpa," I hissed. "You can't say things like that."

This was exactly the type of thing I'd moved to Baker Valley to prevent. Well, okay, I'd had no idea before I moved that my grandpa was capable of pointing a gun at someone and threatening to put them in the ground where they belonged, but he had been slipping lately, and I'd been worried about him all alone now that my grandma was gone.

Barking guy muttered something under his breath as he hiked a slim trail up the mountainside, but at least he was smart enough to keep going and not say it loud enough for my grandpa to hear.

My grandpa followed him with the gun until he finally disappeared from sight, and then returned to the front of the house without another word, waving a hand at our neighbor, Mr. Jackson, on the way. Mr. Jackson nodded back at him and returned to tending his raspberry bushes as if my grandpa threatening someone with a shotgun was a daily occurrence not even worth mentioning.

I hopped off the fence with a loud sigh. Fancy came to check on me and I scratched at her velvety black ears, trying to process what had just happened. "Holy cow, Fancy!" I whispered. "He almost shot that man."

She leaned into my hand with a grumble of pleasure as if to say it was all good now, no harm, no foul.

Was I really the only one that thought it problematic that my grandpa had almost shot someone? I knew I should take the gun away. I mean, you can't have an old man running around pointing a gun at people, no matter how much they might deserve it.

But I was also pretty sure he wasn't just going to hand it over. And I didn't really want the thing. As dangerous as he might be with it, I would be even more so. I'd never handled a gun before and would probably end up shooting myself if I tried. Not to mention, it wasn't the best way to start off my new life living in his house, trying to take his gun away.

Maybe I could skate by with a stern talk this first time

around. And take the gun if it happened again? Oh, that was a good plan.

I trudged back towards the house. "Come on, Fancy. Let's see if we can talk some sense into the most stubborn man I've ever met in my life."

She followed along at my side, tail wagging. I paused to grab my book, wishing I could just sit back down and lose myself in its pages, but I couldn't shirk my commitment, not on my first day of self-appointed grandpa duty.

As I led Fancy inside I comforted myself with the thought that at least he hadn't shot the guy.

"Grandpa?" I called as I pushed through the back door and made my way past the laundry room towards the kitchen.

Fancy shoved ahead of me, her tail wagging a mile a minute as she went to find him. I swear, she loves him ten times more than she loves me. She'd spent the entire night before with her head resting against his feet as we caught up. With me she stays nearby but never actually close enough to touch. Him? She was practically in his lap.

Curse of my life, to own a dog that likes any man more than she likes me.

I found them both in the living room. Grandpa was seated on the worn brown couch he'd owned for at least twenty years, small bits of stuffing pushing out of the tears in the seams. Fancy was leaning against his legs moaning happily as he scratched her ears.

"Where is it?" I demanded, crossing my arms for emphasis as I stared him down.

"Where's what?" He glanced up at me, not the least bit intimidated.

If I hadn't know that he was eighty-two-years-old I would've probably put his age around sixty. He was a trim, tough man who looked like he could take on the world without hesitation, a white t-shirt peeking out from behind a short-sleeved plaid shirt that was tucked into his worn Levi's. Part of the looking younger thing came from the fact that his hair had never grayed, just faded from dark brown to a lighter brown.

I exhaled through my nose, my lips pressed tight together in disapproval. "The gun. You know, the one you just pointed at some stranger walking behind our house?"

"That wasn't a stranger. That was Jack Dunner. Kid's been worthless since the day he was born." He reached for his shirt pocket and then let his hand drop when he remembered he'd stopped smoking three years ago. Too late for my grandma's cancer, but better late than never.

"Well you can't just go pointing a gun at someone because you think they're worthless."

"Look, Maggie May…"

"Maggie, please." It's not easy to be named after a Rod Stewart song, especially when your family insists on using the entire name every time they talk to you.

His lips quirked in a small smile. "Fine, *Maggie*, you have to understand that some people need a little bit more than a firm word to keep them in line. And with a kid like Jack Dunner about the only thing he's going to understand is a punch to the jaw or a shotgun pointed between the eyes. Trust me. I've dealt with plenty of Jack Dunners in my day."

I rolled my eyes. I couldn't help it. Here I was, thirty-six-years-old, rolling my eyes at my grandpa. But, really? I mean, come on. Some people are only going to understand a punch to the jaw or a shotgun pointed between the eyes? Who says things like that? And *believes* them? Because he clearly did.

"Don't you roll your eyes at me, Maggie. You didn't grow up around here, you don't know anything about anybody."

I slumped down on the couch opposite him with an exaggerated sigh, trying not to get stuck as it sagged under my weight. It was a hideous goldenrod color that had probably last been popular in the 70's. Based on the springs poking into my thigh, that was probably how old it was, too.

I tried again. "I didn't grow up here, I'll grant you that. But I can't think of anywhere where it's okay to point a shotgun at someone. You're lucky Mr. Jackson didn't call the cops on you. Or this Jack guy—who is not a kid by the way. He looked to be about twenty-five or so."

"He's a kid to me. Wasn't too long ago I was walking him through how to field a grounder."

My grandpa had been the volunteer coach of the town baseball team for forty years or more. He'd coached every boy and girl in town at one point or another.

"Well maybe you should've worked on his attitude while you were helping him with his fielding instead of having to pull a shotgun on him now."

My grandpa shrugged, reaching for his non-existent cigarettes once more. "Some folks are just born bad, Maggie. Nothing to be done for 'em."

"Oh that's ridiculous. No one is born bad, Grandpa."

I stood. I needed some fresh air. It had been my decision

to move to Baker Valley, but so far things weren't exactly going to plan.

I grabbed my keys. "Look. I need to swing by the store. See how things are going and check in with Jamie. You going to be okay here?"

He snorted. "I think I can manage for a few hours."

"Well just be sure to put that shotgun away, would ya? And try not to shoot anyone while I'm gone?"

"I'll try, but no promises."

I glared at him, but he just winked back at me.

"Come on, Fancy. Let's go."

She glanced up at him before making her slow way to me, making it abundantly clear she'd prefer to stay with him. "You will actually like this, you know, you purebred mutt," I muttered as I put on her leash and collar.

We walked down the front steps to the beat-up van I'd bought just to make Fancy's life easier. I'd loved my old SUV but even at three Fancy already had bad days where it hurt to jump up. And using a ramp? Yeah, no. She jumped over the ramp every single time, making it even worse. So a van it was. I felt like a PTA mom, except my kid was a large black dog who never listened to me.

As Fancy made herself comfortable on the bed that took up half of the back of the van—I'd removed the seats we didn't need—I glanced towards the house, wondering if I'd made a mistake moving to Baker Valley.

It had seemed like such a good idea at the time. I'd live with my grandpa—who wasn't exactly a spring chicken anymore and who'd been all alone since my grandma died two years before. I'd get away from my miserable corporate job and be able to live in one of the most beautiful places I'd ever seen. And, best of all, I'd finally be able to open a business with my best friend from college, Jamie, who was one of the best bakers I knew.

It also gave me a chance to indulge my love of dogs. We were calling the place The Baker Valley Barkery and Café. Get it? Barkery instead of bakery? Because it's a bakery for dogs? At least, half of it is.

(It's alright. Most people don't get it. They keep telling me there's a typo in our logo. I figure someday we'll be famous enough that everyone will know exactly what a barkery is. Until then I'm doomed to multiple conversations about how, no, that really is not a typo, thank you.)

The other half, the café side, was for people. Assuming we ever actually opened. Jamie had been doing all the heavy lifting on getting the place open while I moved. We were two weeks away from opening day, theoretically, but when I'd talked to her the night before she'd told me there had been some "complications" that might delay our opening but not to worry about it, she had it handled.

I'd trust Jamie with my life, but I also knew her well enough to know that when she said there had been complications that might delay the opening that that was Jamiespeak for all hell had broken loose. I needed to see just how bad things were.

As I pulled out of the driveway I figured at least it wasn't going to be worse than my grandpa pointing a shotgun at someone, right?

Wrong.

CHAPTER TWO

By the time I reached the store I'd calmed down enough to see the humor in the whole shotgun situation. It helped that I had a good twenty minute drive to get there. And not through urban sprawl like I was used to, but along a two-lane highway that wound its way through cattle land that was green with spring and dotted with the occasional red barn or one-story ranch home tucked away half a mile off the highway, usually down some rutted dirt road separated from the rest of the world by a rusted metal gate.

The whole area is called Baker Valley because it's a long narrow valley tucked into the Colorado mountains. For tourist trap purposes the towns in the area all agreed to pool their advertising funds and advertise the whole valley, but there are actually a half dozen small towns spread throughout the area. My grandpa's place is at the west end of the valley in a town creatively named Creek that has two gas stations, one church, the county seat, a funeral home, a pioneer museum, and about forty houses, half of which probably started off as mobile homes until someone built a foundation around them.

About ten minutes from there is the town of Masonville. It's where everyone in the valley goes to school and boasts its own McDonald's and a supermarket. (New additions in the last decade. Prior to that folks would drive the hour and half into Denver to stock up on groceries once a month, assuming they didn't live on the deer they hunted and the vegetables they grew in their backyard.)

Another ten minutes past Masonville is the shining jewel of the valley, Bakerstown. (Someone was being awfully creative when they settled the valley, let me tell you. But that was the Colorado settlers for ya. Take your last name and slap it on everything you could find. If that failed, call a spade a spade. So we got Bakerstown for the Baker family, Masonville for the Mason family, and Creek for, you guessed it, the creek that runs through town.)

Bakerstown is the hub of all activity in the valley because it has the ski slopes. Not that most of the locals ski —they're far more interested in snowmobiling—but everyone knows that the skiers are the ones with the money, so the ski slopes are a necessary evil if you want to live somewhere as beautiful as Baker Valley year-round and not live off the land.

And it is beautiful. Picture a sprawling green expanse surrounded on all sides by towering mountains that are covered in evergreens up to the tree line and have snow on the peaks even at the height of summer. Add to that one of the clearest streams you've ever seen running through the whole area like a silver ribbon. (That stream is Fancy's favorite. She loves to go wading and bark at the fishermen there in search of trout.)

I don't know what it is about Baker Valley, but it's always been magic to me. The sky always seems bluer, the clouds— when there are any—are whiter and softer, the air is cleaner, the people are nicer. (For the most part. Not as nice as when I was a little girl who'd come to visit my grandparents for the summer, but still nicer than most of the world.)

I'd never lived full-time in the valley, but it was always where my heart was. And now it was my home, too. All my worries melted away as I drove towards the store, because I was finally where I wanted to be, doing what I wanted to do.

———

That soaring happiness lasted right up to the moment I parked outside our store and noticed the boarded up doors and windows and the black scorch marks on the brick façade.

I sat there, not wanting to go inside and find out why our formerly-pristine building looked like it had been hit by a bomb. I would've probably sat there forever, but Fancy started crying her head off at me to get out of the car.

You'd think a hundred-and-forty-pound dog would have a deep, booming bark but nine times out of ten Fancy resorts to a high-pitched cry that's about as painful on the ears as fingernails on a chalkboard.

It's highly effective, I'll give her that. No one wants to sit in a car with a dog making a noise that obnoxious in their ear. So as much as I wanted to bury my head in my hands and ask, "What now?" I scrambled out of the van and let Fancy out.

Sitting in the car wasn't going to make things better anyway. I needed to find out what Jamie had kept from me and hope it wasn't so bad we'd have to delay our opening. All of my plans hinged on being open that first weekend in June.

Something that did not look very likely at the moment.

CHAPTER THREE

I walked Fancy to the grass at the far end of the parking lot and turned back to look at the store. The little cartoon Newfie heads on either end of the sign made me smile—they'd been my idea, in honor of Fancy. In between, in the curly script the sign guy hadn't wanted to use, it proclaimed this as the home of the Baker Valley Barkery and Café.

(I'll admit, it was a little hard to read, but I thought it had flare. Better than using Helvetica like he'd suggested. How boring would that have been?)

The café was on the left, the barkery on the right, each with their own door and large picture window that would give guests a great view of the mountains—once the cheap plywood that was currently covering them was removed, that is. If I hadn't known better, I would've thought a hurricane was coming, the way the windows were boarded over. But this was Colorado, so clearly something else had happened since my last visit.

Inside there should be tables set up on both sides with a pass-through that would allow someone on the café side to access the barkery side and vice versa. There was a lot less seating on the barkery side than the café side because we wanted to leave enough room for dogs as well as humans to sit comfortably.

We'd also added little cubbies surrounded by half-walls on the barkery side where people could leave their dogs safely for a few minutes while they ran to the restroom. (I've been that person traveling cross-country with their dog who just needs to pee real quick but doesn't want to leave their dog in a hot car while they do, so I can appreciate the need to have a safe space like that.)

My space—the service counter of the barkery—was at the far back on the right-hand side. We had one of those glass display cases like any good bakery would, but all of the treats were going to be for dogs instead of humans. Fancy's favorite were the Doggie Delights—which were basically balls of peanut butter with other yummy stuff added in— but she was only allowed one per day. Those calories add up fast, and a big girl like her needs to watch the stress she puts on her joints.

Fancy's personal cubby—which was big enough for an extra-large dog bed and her food and water bowls—was in the far corner behind the barkery counter.

Opposite that was our dogphenalia section that included Baker Valley leashes and collars, mugs with a circular version of our logo, those dog window stickers everyone loves, and whatever other kitschy items I thought might sell to a dog-loving tourist crowd.

There were also some pre-packaged treat bags I'd had

manufactured so people could take them home as gifts for their furry friends who hadn't made the trip. (If you ever want to know how private label packaging works, just ask. I know more about it now than I ever wanted to.) And just in case we didn't attract enough visitors to the store, I was also planning on offering everything via our website, too.

I wanted to make it as easy for people to give me their money as I could.

The opposite side of the store was Jamie's side. It was a regular café that was going to serve things like coffee and cinnamon rolls. (Jamie makes the best cinnamon rolls in the world. I kid you not. They are better than any cinnamon roll I have ever tasted and I have made it my life's mission to try cinnamon rolls everywhere I go.) The café side included a full kitchen and a small office that were kept completely separate from the barkery side.

Let me tell you, negotiating everything with the local zoning inspector had been a challenge. He was full of what-if scenarios. What if two dogs were seated too close to each other and got in a fight? What if someone tripped over a dog trying to get to their table? What if dog hair made its way into the human food? What if, what if, what if.

We'd met every single objection and then some, and I was proud of what we'd built, but now, looking at the scorch marks on the bricks around the windows and doors, I was a little scared to step through that door.

No point in delaying, though. Best to see what had happened and figure out how to deal with it. I led Fancy across the lot, forcing myself to take deep, calming breaths. Jamie was alive and well. We still had two weeks. It was going to be okay.

Jamie met me at the door, wiping the sweat from her face with a hand still covered in a thick leather workman's glove. She'd braided her long brown hair back, but little tendrils had escaped and were fuzzed around her face.

As she pulled the gloves off her slender fingers and tucked them into the back pocket of her jeans, I asked, "Do I want to know what happened here?"

"It's fine. Nothing to worry about. I've got it under control."

I've never seen Jamie ruffled. You could put her in the middle of a total apocalypse and she'd look around with a shrug and say, "Well, best get to it. Things aren't going to fix themselves." It's what makes her such a great business partner. Always dependable, competent as all get out, and never willing to admit defeat.

But this time I had to wonder if she'd lost her connection to reality. There were black soot marks on the ceiling on the café side and it was clear that all of the glass in the windows and doors had been violently removed by a significant amount of force. A sooty smell hung in the air and Fancy sneezed twice, shaking her head.

I glanced towards the kitchen which was a soot-stained mess from the little bit I could see. "It's fine?"

"A minor setback, that's all." Jamie bent down to say hi to Fancy while I pressed my lips together and counted to ten, reminding myself that if Jamie said she had it handled, she probably did.

We'd known each other since we were babies and I'd come to the valley to visit my grandparents, but we hadn't become life-long friends until freshman year of college at CU when we found ourselves on a volunteer project to repaint a local elementary school. The thing was a disaster. There was paint, thankfully, but that was about it. No paint-brushes. No drop cloths. No one who knew a thing about anything.

Jamie and I both stepped up at the same moment to take things in hand. Within an hour we had all the supplies we needed and four teams hard at work. We'd been best friends ever since. And after years of complaining to one another about how miserable we were working for people who didn't see what we could and commiserating over how much we missed the valley, we'd decided enough was enough, pooled our savings, and decided to open the barkery and cafe.

Things *had* been going well.

"So?" I asked.

Jamie shrugged one shoulder. "We didn't get the gas on the stove in the café hooked up the way it should've been and there was a bit of an explosion."

"A bit of an explosion? Was anyone hurt?"

"No. It was just Katie and me working at the time." She nodded towards a young woman with bright red hair pulled back in a ponytail and the most flawless porcelain skin I'd ever seen in my life who was hard at work scrubbing down the floor. "Luckily the gas buildup wasn't near as bad as it could've been because I'd propped open the front door to let in some fresh air, so the explosion took out all the glass and knocked me for a loop, but that was it."

"Jamie! Why didn't you tell me?"

"Because I had it under control and there was nothing you could do about it from wherever you were that day.

Would you have really left Fancy and your U-Haul truck in Lexington, Kentucky so you could fly back here and check on me? No. And I wouldn't have wanted you to. I knew you'd be here in a few days and I could tell you then."

I eyed her up and down. "No broken bones?"

"No."

The way she answered made me narrow my eyes and study her more closely. "Concussion?"

"Just a minor one. I'll have a few extra headaches for a while, that's it."

I glanced towards the girl scrubbing the floor who was now trying to keep Fancy at bay. Clearly not a dog person the way she was grimacing and shoving at Fancy. "And Katie?"

"She was outside when it happened, so no injuries there, thankfully. Kitchen took the brunt of it."

"Fancy, leave the girl alone," I called as I headed for the kitchen. Fancy came to join me, Jamie trailing along behind us.

I stopped at the entrance to the kitchen. The walls and the ceiling were almost completely black and what looked like part of the stove was still embedded in the wall to my left. The burnt smell was almost overpowering and Fancy backed away pawing at her nose.

"Here, Fancy." I opened the door next to the kitchen and let her out into the dog run we'd had built out back. She went eagerly, but then turned back to stare at me plaintively when I didn't follow her outside.

I turned back to Jamie. "It could've killed you."

"But it didn't." She flashed me one of her signature smiles. "I'm lucky. You know that."

I shook my head. She was lucky—as this incident proved yet again—but still. That didn't mean she had to be cavalier about it. What if she'd been in the kitchen when this happened? What if she hadn't propped the door open?

I shivered, trying not to think about it. "Are you going to sue the idiot who messed the gas line up?"

"No. And neither are you. It was just a freak accident. No one needs to be sued over it. Everything's going to be fixed in time for our launch and that's all that matters."

I glanced back at the kitchen. "We're launching in two weeks and that's going to be fixed in time?"

"Luke promised me he'll take care of it and I trust he will."

"Luke, huh?" I stepped closer, holding her gaze. "Is this the same Luke who broke your heart at least once a year from third grade through high school and then at least twice in college? Mr. Honeyed Words and Hollow Promises?"

She crossed her arms and glared me down. "He's the best general contractor in the area. He'll get it done. Trust me."

I wanted to argue—the fact that Luke was involved did not bode well—but I bit my tongue and let it go. Jamie was blind where Luke was concerned and the last thing I needed was a big blow up fight with my best friend and business partner two weeks before our launch.

I just hoped she was right about him getting everything done in time. There was a big dog show that was going to be held at the local convention center in two weeks, and if we weren't open in time for that I wasn't sure how the barkery was going to get the word of mouth buzz it needed to succeed. The café side would probably survive a late opening, but the barkery? I didn't think it would.

While Jamie and I had been talking, Fancy had wandered back over to Katie, muddy paw prints showing her wandering trail from the back door to Katie's side.

"Sorry about Fancy," I called to her. "I'll clean that up in a minute. By the way, I'm Maggie." I leaned across the counter and held out my hand.

She stood, clearly not wanting to, and took my hand. "Katie."

Her handshake was about as warm as her non-existent smile and she barely made eye contact before looking away. I studied her as she made her way behind the counter and into the kitchen area, face completely blank of emotion. It's always fascinated me when I meet a really attractive person who's like that. I always wonder how someone can get such positive attention from the world—because with skin like that *and* red hair you know men had to bow and scrape around her all the time—and yet come out so…meh.

My own looks—tall, blonde, and curvy enough to get some attention—had certainly made my life easier. Maybe I could see being shut down with men, because it could be too much sometimes, but all the time? It was just weird.

Jamie, knowing this particular fascination of mine, distracted me by handing me a Coke from the little mini fridge under the counter. "Katie is Georgia's daughter. You remember, Georgia, right?"

"The one who liked to eat mud?" I whispered.

"That's the one."

I gave Jamie my "what were you thinking?" look but she just shrugged. She loves to collect strays and help "fix" them. I figure that's what explains her lifelong fascination with Luke.

"Katie will be with us through next summer and then it's off to college. Right, Katie?" she asked as Katie returned, a mop in hand.

Katie faced off against Fancy, the mop gripped in her hands like a bat. "That's my mother's plan."

I stepped between them and waved a treat under Fancy's nose, luring her to her cubbie behind the barkery counter so I could lock her out of Katie's way before something bad happened. Fancy hesitated for a second—she didn't want to leave the action—but treats always win with her, even when they're the size of a peanut.

You'd think a dog her size would need big treats, but nope, not at all. She'll follow you anywhere for a crumb of a crumb of a crumb.

I settled Fancy down and returned to the café counter, careful to keep out of Katie's way. "And what do you want, Katie?" I asked, genuinely curious and determined to break through that cold exterior. I figured she had to have some hidden passion, right? Everyone does, even if it's stamp collecting.

"I don't know." The way she said it made it pretty clear she was done talking to me. And the abuse she was inflicting on that mop and floor were enough for me to just leave her to it. She didn't want to talk, fine with me.

I turned back to Jamie. "You would not believe what my grandpa did this morning..."

I walked her through the whole crazy incident while Katie worked around us, violently cleaning the floor until it shone. Jamie laughed so hard when I told her about my grandpa pulling his shotgun, I thought she was going to hurt herself.

I grinned. "It was pretty funny, wasn't it?"

"Oh yeah. And your grandpa's right, you know. There isn't much that will get through to a man like Jack Dunner, but I bet that shotgun woke him up and made him pay attention."

"It certainly woke me up, I'll tell you that."

"Can I go?" Katie interrupted us.

Jamie blinked at her, clearly surprised, but then nodded. "Sure. See you tomorrow?"

"Yeah." She dumped the mop in the kitchen and left without so much as a smile or wave.

"That is one odd girl," I muttered as she revved the engine on an old blue pickup truck and backed out of her parking spot.

"Yeah, well, her mom keeps her on a pretty tight leash. Doesn't want Katie to end up like her, you know."

"How old was she when she had her first kid?"

"Fifteen."

"And how old is Katie?"

"Seventeen."

I shrugged. "She's already done better than her mom then, yeah?"

"Yeah, tell that to Georgia. She wants Katie to avoid all boys until she's at college and maybe even after that."

I winced. "That's not going to work out well…"

"No, it's not. So when Katie asks to leave a little early or come in a little late every once in a while, I let her. Kid's gotta be a kid, you know."

"Hm. Well, when that backfires, you can deal with

Georgia. Woman scares me. Always has." I went to let Fancy out of her cubbie, but she was sound asleep, sprawled on her back, her right paw sticking straight up in the air. Goofy girl.

"It's just a half hour here or there. No big deal." Jamie looked at Fancy and shook her head, smiling.

"A person can do a lot in half an hour, you know." We walked back to the café side and I grabbed a wash rag to start wiping down the tables that all had a fine layer of soot on them. "By the way, does Katie get friendlier the more you know her?"

Jamie smacked me in the arm. "Be nice, Maggie. It's hard to be a teenager."

I guessed, but I sure hoped she'd warm up soon, because she was not my idea of the ideal café employee. I'd have to stash her in the back and help all the customers myself if she didn't warm up, which sort of defeated the whole purpose of having her around.

Ah well. I glanced at the burned out kitchen. One disgruntled unfriendly teenager was the least of my worries.

CHAPTER FOUR

THE DAY BEFORE THE STORE OPENING DAWNED BLUE AND beautiful, like most days in early spring in the Colorado mountains. Fortunately for me, the last two weeks had passed without any exploding stoves or reports of my grandpa pointing a shotgun at someone new. I'd spent most of the time with Fancy, Jamie, and Katie Cross—who'd grown on me some, but not much—getting the store ready for our opening.

Luke had come through for us, just like Jamie said he would. He was still an over-the-top flirtatious sleazeball who was going to break my best friend's heart—again—but at least by the day before the opening we had a fully-functional store that didn't show a single sign of fire damage.

I had plans that day to go into the store and make sure everything was perfect for our launch, but not until after noon. Poor Fancy had put up with a lot of long hours sleeping in her nook at the store and I figured she'd earned a little hike in the woods before opening day.

Not that I really thought she minded all that time snoring away in the corner. She is a Newfie after all and Newfs aren't exactly the most energetic of breeds. But I knew she also liked to get out and smell new things and we really hadn't had a chance to do so since our arrival.

So after I fed her breakfast at five-thirty in the morning —an unfortunate side effect of living those first crucial months of her life in an apartment with a neighbor who had a loud alarm and liked to get up at that time every morning of every day—we headed up the mountain behind my grandpa's house.

Most of the mountainside was covered not only with big evergreens and tightly-clustered aspens, but with juniper bushes and long grass that you wouldn't want to try to walk through. Fortunately for us, there was a nice little trail I'd seen Mr. Jackson tending the day of our arrival that was just wide enough for me and Fancy to walk side-by-side. Mr. Jackson had done a good job of cutting back the branches, because not one slapped me in the face as we made our way towards the ridgeline about five hundred feet above my grandpa's house.

Fancy's a good girl so she didn't pull on her leash at all, just stopped to sniff and pee on things every few feet. She sometimes became a little too focused on one spot or another and I had to tell her to leave it and give a slight tug to move along, but usually I just let her do her thing. The walk was as much for her as it was for me, after all.

It was a gorgeous late spring morning. Birds were singing in the trees, bees were buzzing around on the early wildflowers scattered along the mountainside, and everything smelled fresh and clean and alive.

I was winded within five minutes because I wasn't used to hiking up mountainsides, and certainly not at seven thousand feet, but that was okay. It was worth it to feel like no one else in the world existed for just a little bit, especially knowing how stressful things would be once the store actually opened.

I probably should've thought about bears or mountain lions or criminals living in caves, but I didn't. I'd always thought of the mountain as part of my grandpa's home. Hardly anybody went there so it was easy to think of it as an extension of his backyard.

I took a break on a large rock slab most of the way up the mountainside. It was big enough it created a perfect space for sitting and watching the sleepy little town below us. I could just barely hear the freight train that passed through town down by the creek on its way to some unknown destination. When we were little, Jamie and I would go up there to watch the trains while we munched on peach slices sprinkled with sugar that her mom had put in a plastic baggie for us.

(It's a wonder neither one of us has diabetes or serious weight issues, the way we used to eat.)

Fancy sprawled out on the ground next to the rock, content to let me have my moment. She was snoring away within moments.

I took a deep breath. Tomorrow was the day. Tomorrow we'd open the Barkery and Café and see if this crazy little dream of ours had any hope of succeeding.

I was scared. Scared that I'd finally chosen to risk everything and pursue my dream and that I'd fail. Scared that I'd have to go back to living in the city, driving an hour each way to work, spending all day everyday inside while the sun shone outside, arguing with people about things that probably didn't matter to anyone but us.

I'd never held it against the folks that liked that sort of thing, but for me that rock in the middle of a mountainside had always been where I'd wanted to be. Right there, looking down at the peaceful little town that was my home, my dog at my side.

It had taken longer to get there than I'd wanted, but I was finally making it happen.

I just hoped it would work out...

After a while, Fancy got restless. Or at least her version of restless, which involved her giving me what I like to call her puppy side-eye where she looks at me out of the corner of her eye like, "Are we done yet? Can we go do something interesting now?" and cries really softly.

If I ignore her, she'll stop. She's good that way. She's learned over the years that sometimes I just have to do my work and she has to be patient until I'm done. But if I show the slightest weakness, she won't let up.

Since the hike was as much for her as for me, we moved on after her first little cry. We continued to the ridgeline where we could see a gorgeous valley nestled between four separate mountain peaks. I'd always loved that valley as a kid; it was so pristine and untouched, nestled there where no one could find it, a secret little hideaway.

I narrowed my eyes at the small wooden cabin that now stood at one end of the valley, rows of something growing nearby. We were too far away for me to tell what was being grown down there, but I figured I had a pretty good idea. Just because Colorado had legalized pot didn't mean that private grow operations had gone away. It wasn't my scene, as a user or a grower, but I'd heard that some folks still grew their own despite the laws.

I turned away from the valley, disappointed to see a treasured childhood memory tarnished that way, even though I'd known it was inevitable. Everything beautiful and private is eventually discovered and destroyed. Still makes me sad when it happens, though.

Reminding myself that the forest around me was still a thousand times more beautiful than the concrete streets of most major cities, I nudged Fancy farther along the ridgeline, determined to enjoy it while I could.

Fancy tugged at her leash and glanced back at me, pleading silently for me to let her run free. I debated doing it. She's good at staying nearby, so I didn't figure she'd run away or anything. But I still remembered that one time at Elk Meadow when she'd seen a couple elk and left me for a good ten minutes while she chased them. I'd been convinced that was the end until I heard her crying her little heart out trying to find me.

I wasn't going to take that kind of risk again, no matter how much she wanted to go exploring. Instead I let her tug me along the trail, her nose pressed tight to the ground as she followed some scent I couldn't detect.

Not until the end that is. Dead things have a certain common stench all their own. Not that I'd known that before I had a dog. But once I got Fancy and we started going to big outdoor dog parks I'd soon learned all about the smell of dead things.

She loves them. We'll be walking along just fine and then there she'll go, off into the bushes, and I'll come up to find her peeing on something that reeks of death. A badger, a squirrel, a rabbit. You name it, she's peed on it.

That's nature for you. Things die, and when they do, they stink. And when they stink, dogs like to pee on them. It's the circle of life. Or so I tell myself.

And trying to keep Fancy from a dead thing once she's found it is almost impossible. I'm not a small woman— about five-eight, one-sixty—but there's no way I can hold back a hundred-and-forty-pound dog who's built for pulling things when she's determined to go somewhere.

So I turned my face away as we got close and let her do her peeing thing. (Thankfully, she's only tried to roll in dead things twice and both times they were fish, so no worries she'd do that this time.)

When she'd finished, I tugged on her leash. "Come on, Fancy, let's go."

She wouldn't budge. I started to worry maybe she really was going to roll in this one and pulled harder. "Come on, Fancy."

I grabbed her collar and pulled her back, but she fought me for every step. "Darn it, Fancy. What's so special about this one?" I demanded.

I almost fell on my butt in surprise when I looked past her and saw what she'd been peeing on. Because it wasn't a badger or a squirrel or a rabbit.

It was a man. And not just any man, but that crazy man who'd barked at me the day after I arrived. At least, I thought it was. Maybe. Stupid ballcap was the same. Hair color looked to be, too.

I stepped closer to take another look, burying my nose in my elbow to try to mask the scent. Somehow I'd been fine when I thought it was a small rodent I was smelling, but now that I knew it was dead human I wanted nothing to do with it.

Of course, Fancy thought my stepping closer was an invitation to pee on him again…Sigh.

It was a little hard to tell if it was him, because the body was mostly buried under some old leaves, but it certainly looked like him. I was tempted, just for a moment, to move the leaves out of the way to check. Call it morbid curiosity —I'd never seen a dead person who hadn't died in a hospital before. I knew these kinds of things happened, but never in my world.

Fortunately, I'd watched enough crime scene shows on television to know I didn't want to mess with the scene or get my DNA all mixed up with his, so I dragged Fancy far enough along the trail to get away from the immediate smell of him while I tried to figure out what to do next.

CHAPTER FIVE

THE OBVIOUS CHOICE WHEN YOU FIND A DEAD BODY IS TO call the cops. Maybe the guy had just been mauled by a bear or something and that's all there'd be to it. Just a "Howdya do, there's a dead body on that trail up there that someone needs to take care of" and I could be on my merry way.

But...

My grandpa *had* threatened him with a shotgun. Not that I really thought my grandpa was capable of tracking a man up a mountainside, gunning him down, and burying his body under dead leaves.

Not really.

I mean...No. He'd had a rough early life, but he was past all that now.

At least, I thought he was.

But what if he wasn't? What if he really had followed this guy up the mountain and gunned him down? Sure, I believed that murder was wrong and people should do their time and all that. But my grandpa? He was old. He didn't deserve to go to prison. (Again.) Not at his age.

So letting a little more time pass until someone else discovered the body made a certain amount of sense to me. Maybe by then Mr. Jackson would've forgotten the little confrontation he'd witnessed or at least be a little more fuzzy on the details.

I know. I'm a horrible person. But this was family we were talking about.

There was also the hassle factor. Did I really want to call the cops and get all mixed up in them finding a dead body the day before I was supposed to open my new store? They'd probably want to question me. And who knew how long that would take.

Everything at the store was ready to go—Jamie and I weren't the kind of people to leave things to the last minute —but still. I didn't want to spend most of my last day of freedom in an interview room waiting to be questioned about the death of some jerk who'd barked at me.

Not to mention the gossip factor. This was a small town. People would know I'd found the body and that's all they'd want to talk about. I didn't want to ruin our opening with thoughts of dead people under bushes. Talk about unappetizing.

(I really am a horrible person, aren't I?)

But then I figured he probably had a mother who was missing him by now and who deserved to know that he wouldn't be home for Christmas. And what if he had kids? Didn't they deserve to know where their daddy was?

While I debated and thought things through, Fancy lay down on the path. (She's not one for standing if she doesn't have to.) As I processed all the pros and cons she rested her head on her paws and watched me with her steady amber gaze, her mind already made up.

"Fine," I sighed and reached for my phone. "See? Happy now?"

She sighed and closed her eyes while I dialed 9-1-1.

Luckily for the dead guy, I had enough of a signal to complete the call, because if I'd had to walk back down the mountain first, I probably would've rethought my decision. But no, the call went through just fine. I explained to the very sweet and patient woman who answered exactly what I'd found.

I'm not sure she believed me—Creek isn't exactly a hotbed of criminal activity—but she took down my information and told me an officer would be by my grandpa's to talk to me after they'd checked out my story.

Good enough. I'd done my civic duty. If they decided it was a prank call, fine by me, I'd just be sure not to let Fancy close enough to pee on the body next time we were in the area.

I stomped my way back down the mountainside to my grandpa's, Fancy trotting along in front of me happily sniffing anything and everything, tail wagging with joy.

At least one of us was having a good day.

———

When I got back home I told my grandpa what had happened, watching his face for any sign he already knew. His only reaction was to reach for his non-existent cigarettes and say, "Someone was going to shoot that man sooner or later. Only question was who," and then turn his attention back to the daily crossword.

I didn't want to freak Jamie out the day before the opening so I just texted her that something had come up and I'd try to be in later but didn't know when. She immediately thought something had happened to my grandpa and I had to text her back to let her know no one was hurt or injured. Or at least, no one that mattered. When she texted a "???" to that, I just let her know that I'd give her the full story once I got there.

Whenever that was.

And then I waited. And waited. And waited.

I had a book I'd been enjoying, but my mind was so distracted I stopped trying to read it after I read the same paragraph ten times and still couldn't remember what it said.

I tried grilling my grandpa about the dead guy, but he told me to leave him alone. (He takes his crossword puzzles very seriously. Even has a crossword dictionary he carries around like other people carry a bible. And doesn't appreciate if you look over his shoulder while trying to find something to do and solve one of the answers for him either, let me tell you.)

I was tempted to start looking the dead guy up on the internet but then decided that probably wasn't the best of ideas. What if the cops seized my computer and saw all those searches? What would they think?

(Probably nothing, I know. But you try finding a dead body behind your house and then waiting for the cops to come by and see what you come up with to entertain yourself while you're waiting.)

Finally, when I was about at my wit's end and ready to just head out to the store for something to do, there was a knock at our front door.

"I've got it." I raced to answer the door while my grandpa grunted a reply without even bothering to look up from his crossword. Fancy lifted her head halfway from where she was lying at his feet and then dropped back to the ground with a loud sigh. (She's not the best of guard dogs...)

I yanked open the front door—it sticks but I maybe gave it a little more force than it needed in my excitement—to find a very good-looking man in a cop's uniform, hand raised to knock again. He was tall, dark hair, blue eyes, and filled out his uniform in a very pleasing sort of way.

I gave myself two seconds to appreciate an example of the beauty this world has to offer and then I shut all that nonsense down, because I had a business to start up, a grandpa to take care of, and a dead body to discuss.

"Bout time you got here," I said. I knew I was being rude, but he'd made me wait a long time. Plus good-looking men make me cranky. I don't like being distracted.

He grinned at me in that way overly-confident men sometimes have. "Maggie May. It's been a long time."

I glared at him. I'd remember knowing a man who looked like that. And I didn't. "I'm sorry, am I supposed to know you?"

My grandpa, who'd finally bothered to join us, squeezed my shoulder. "Now, Maggie May, is that any way to treat your first love?" He shook the man's hand. "Women. How quickly they forget. How've you been, Matt?"

Matt—whoever that was—shook my grandpa's hand with a firm grip and slight nod. "Good, Mr. Carver. I'm at my dad's old place. Getting all his stuff sorted and taken care of."

"And the new job? You're liking it?"

He shrugged one shoulder. "It's not as exciting as Iraq."

"Not much is, I'm sure. That a good thing or a bad thing?"

He thought for a moment. "Both."

My grandpa laughed and I crossed my arms, glaring at both of them. "If you two are done catching up? I assume you're here about the dead body?"

"I am." He grinned at me, the smile wrinkles in the corners of his eyes giving him a mischievous look that was a little too appealing.

"Let me get my shoes and I'll show you where it is."

"No need. We already found him. I left Sue up there doing her thing so I could come down, welcome you to the neighborhood, and get your statement."

"Who's Sue? And why do you think you know me? I'd… remember if we'd met."

He laughed. He had a good laugh, but I shoved that thought away as fast as it occurred to me.

"Sue is the coroner. She's taking her pictures and seeing to the body. And we have met. Many, many years ago. I lived in Creek before my mom moved us to Bakerstown. According to her, you and I were inseparable."

My grandpa chuckled. "You two *were* adorable together. Of course, I can't say I appreciated how Maggie chose to demonstrate her affection for you." He pointed at the wall behind me where the word Matt was scrawled in permanent black marker, twelve-inches high, the letters poorly-formed and wobbly. "Thirty years and I've never been able to remove that no matter how hard I try."

I flushed scarlet. "You're *that* Matt?"

"Yep. Sure am."

My grandpa laughed. "You want me to drag out the photo of the two of you cuddled together in my armchair reading a book? It really is a great picture."

Fortunately, Fancy chose that moment to introduce herself. She nudged Matt's hand with her nose, demanding his attention.

"Hey, there, who do we have here?" he asked as he knelt down and started rubbing her ears. She groaned in pleasure and practically knocked him over as she leaned into him, eyes closed in ecstasy. I was grateful for the save, but disgusted by how easily she let him win her over. Sellout.

I headed for the kitchen, desperately in need of a Coke. This day was not going at all the way I'd planned it. At least Fancy redeemed herself when Officer Handsome tried to follow me to the kitchen. She wove her way between his legs like an oversized cat and almost tripped him. I smiled. Something needed to bring that man down a notch or ten. He was far too confident for his own good.

Of course, he just laughed. Points to him for being a dog person, but a man who was handsome *and* a dog person was so not what I needed right then.

CHAPTER SIX

THE THREE OF US SETTLED AT THE KITCHEN TABLE, A small metal table shoved up against the wall, leaving only three possible places to sit. My grandpa picked up his crossword and pretended to be working on it, but I knew he was listening to every word we said.

Matt opened the Coke I'd given him, the sound of its fizzing filling the air between us. He said there was no need for a formal interview down at the station. Unless I'd killed the guy, that is.

After confirming that no, I had not killed the man, left his body there to rot, and then gone back to report it later, we got started. The first few questions were simple enough. Name. Address. Age. Marital Status. I raised an eyebrow at that last one but answered Single and moved on like it was nothing worth noting.

Then he asked me how I'd found the body.

I'd debated this one while I was waiting for him to arrive. Should I tell the cop my dog peed on the dead body before I realized what it was? Or should I just keep that to myself and let him assume any pee on the body was from wild animals? Because they'd have to notice, right? I mean, that kind of thing leaves something behind. And on all those cop shows they always are able to tell who the pee belonged to

I mean, okay, not like they're going around testing pee all the time on those shows. But often enough that it's come up as the one little thing that gets the killer busted in the end at least once or twice. I wouldn't want them going down the wrong path only to find out it was my dog that had done it.

So after taking an extra swallow of Coke, I told him what Fancy had done. Both he and my grandpa stared at me.

"What?" I said, defensively. "Don't look at me like that. She likes to pee on dead things. She's a dog."

Matt glanced at Fancy who was sound asleep under the table, her head nestled against his foot, traitor that she was. "You don't look like you like to pee on dead things," he told her.

"She has hidden depths."

He laughed softly. "So I see. You didn't know she was peeing on a body?"

"No. I wasn't looking. I could smell it, but I don't like to look too closely at the dead things she pees on."

He scrawled a series of notes on his notepad. I tried to see what he was writing—I'm pretty good at reading upside down—but his handwriting was completely illegible.

He noticed and turned his notes towards me. "Short hand. My grandma taught me. You'd be amazed how much knowing it has come in handy over the years."

Ah. That explained it. He was cheating. I made a mental note to learn short hand. I don't like not knowing what someone is writing about me. Not that we were ever going to cross paths again, not if I could help it.

"That all you need?" I asked, ready for him to leave and never come back.

"Almost. Did you know him?"

I bounced my Coke can against the table, trying to figure out how to answer his question. "You mean, had we been introduced?"

He narrowed his eyes. "Sure. Let's start there."

"No, we had not." I beamed at him, pretty pleased with how I'd side-stepped that landmine.

He leaned closer and I felt like the overhead kitchen light had suddenly been transformed into one of those police interrogation lamps. "Did you know who he was when you found the body?"

"I had my suspicions." I held his intense blue gaze, refusing to crack.

"How so? If you hadn't been introduced?"

I bit my lip, trying to figure out how to step around the question. The only sound in the kitchen was the tap, tap, tap of my Coke can on the tabletop as I tried to find an answer that wouldn't implicate my grandpa.

Unfortunately, he did it for me.

"Oh for heaven's sake, Maggie May, just tell the man." He turned to Matt. "The day after Maggie arrived, Jack went walking up the trail behind our house, and when Fancy here barked at him he barked back at her. So Maggie told him what for and he barked at her, too."

Matt nodded. "Okay. What was so hard about that?"

"Because Maggie probably thinks I shot him."

"Grandpa!" I pressed my lips together and bugged my eyes out in the universal sign for keep your mouth shut, but he wasn't even looking at me.

"And why would she think that, Mr. Carver?"

My grandpa reached for his non-existent cigarettes and cussed softly when he remembered he didn't smoke anymore.

"Sir?"

"Because I threatened him with my shotgun. You know how that boy was, words were never enough."

"Grandpa," I hissed. "You didn't have to tell him that."

Matt raised an eyebrow at me and I sat back in my chair, feeling only slightly guilty for encouraging my grandpa to lie to the police.

My grandpa looked right at me as he added, "I didn't shoot him, by the way. Not worth the lead. Especially when someone else was going to do it sooner rather than later."

Matt tapped his pen on his paper. "I believe you, sir, but that puts me in an awfully awkward position."

"Why's that?"

"Because it looks like Jack was shot with a shotgun. At least that's Sue's preliminary."

"Well, I didn't do it. Lots of people in this town own shotguns. Now, if you'd found the body on my front yard, maybe you could think it was me. But not halfway up the mountainside. I'm too old to go tracking someone down like that."

Matt pinched the bridge of his nose. It was clear he believed my grandpa but he was also a man of the law and he couldn't just ignore such a likely suspect. "Do you have the gun, sir?"

"Of course I do." My grandpa crossed his arms and glared at Matt like he'd just proven himself to be a little low in the intelligence department.

Matt didn't even flinch. "Is it locked up tight in a gun safe?"

My grandpa snorted. "What good would that do me? Take me ten minutes to get the stupid thing out and by then I'd be dead or the trouble would be gone."

I winced. I wasn't surprised, but I really, really wished he hadn't said that.

Matt made a note on his notepad. "So your shotgun, which you swear you did not use to kill Jack Dunner, is somewhere in this house but not locked up?"

"No. It's in my truck."

I almost fell out of my chair. Seriously? He'd left a shotgun in his truck?

"Is the truck locked?" Matt asked, his tone making it clear he already knew what the answer to that was going to be.

"No. This is Creek, not some big fancy city. I don't need to lock my truck."

"Grandpa..." I buried my face in my hands. Did he honestly not understand how problematic it was that he was carrying a loaded gun around in an unlocked truck? Set aside the fact that a man had been murdered with a weapon just like that, he had to know it was never a good idea to leave a loaded gun just lying around.

Didn't he?

Matt nodded once. "Okay. I'm going to need to see that gun, sir."

"See it or take it?" My grandpa leveled a look at Matt that had backed down more than one dangerous man over the years.

"Both." Matt met him glare for glare, which I had to reluctantly admit was pretty impressive. "If you'd had it locked in your gun safe, maybe I could've left it with you. But you're telling me that you had an unsecured firearm sitting in a vehicle anyone could've accessed within the vicinity of a murder. I have to consider that your gun, whether you shot it or not, was the murder weapon."

My grandpa huffed a laugh. "Fine. Take it. But you better bring it back to me as soon as you're done with it."

"So you can point it at someone else who upsets you?" Matt asked with a smile.

"Now you listen here, Matthew Allen Barnes, I knew you before you could toddle. And you will not make smart aleck comments to me like that. I am a responsible gun owner and I want my gun back once you see that I didn't use it to kill someone. Got it?"

"Yes, sir." Matt downed the rest of his Coke and set it back on the table. There was still a faint smile on his lips. "Maggie, it was nice to see you again after all these years. Mr. Carver, if you'll lead me to the gun?"

As they walked to the door I hoped that would be the last of it. Unfortunately, the way things had been going so far, I suspected Officer Barnes would be back sooner rather than later.

Just what I needed.

CHAPTER SEVEN

IT WAS ALMOST A RELIEF TO GO TO THE BARKERY AFTER that morning's excitement. Jamie had brought in her golden retriever puppy, Lulu, and we let Fancy and Lulu run around in the dog run out back while I filled her in on all the details.

"You don't think he really did it, do you?" she asked.

"No. He couldn't have. I mean, okay, he probably *could* have, but he wouldn't have. Like he told the cop, waste of lead."

Luke, general contractor and all around pain in my, well, you know, poked his head out the barkery door. "Hey, Beautiful. Hey, Sunshine. How are you ladies doing today?"

I rolled my eyes and ignored him. I'd learned long ago that any man who calls all women by little names like that all the time is a player. You don't have to keep track of who you're flirting with if every woman is Beautiful or Sunshine.

Unfortunately, Jamie had never learned the same lesson. (As her string of unfortunate boyfriends showed). "Hey,

Luke," she simpered at him. "I thought you guys were done with all your work."

As he stepped onto the back patio I caught a peek of Katie staring forlornly at him before the door closed. Not her, too. What was it about the man? Sure, he was good-looking in that rugged cowboy/bad boy sort of way. You just knew he'd suggest going skinny dipping in some private pond tucked away on a bit of property he didn't own given even a little bit of encouragement. But, really. Couldn't they see through his crap?

He leaned against the wall and leered down at us. (Okay, I call it leering. Jamie would've called it smiling and wouldn't have noticed the way he angled himself for the best view down her shirt.)

"I figured I'd drop by, give things one last look, and maybe give my ladies a little kiss on the cheek for good luck." He had the audacity to wink at us.

Jamie giggled. I stood up. "I'm good, thanks. And you just remember that that red-headed beauty inside is too young for you to be giving kisses to, you hear me?" I glared at him.

"Who, Katie? She's seventeen. That's not too young."

"Yes, it is. You go anywhere near that girl in that way and you will answer to me. Got it?"

He shrugged me off. "You don't have to be such a buzzkill, Maggie. She'll be eighteen in two more months."

I glared him down. I hadn't missed the fact that he knew exactly how old she was and exactly when he could make a move on her without repercussions. At least of the legal variety.

Jamie looked up at him, a slight frown on her face. "Are

you attracted to Katie?" Her voice trembled. Great, just what I needed. A love triangle between my best friend, the resident sleaze, and our shop assistant.

Luke leaned in and brushed his hand down the side of Jamie's face. "She's a pretty girl, that's all. Not a beautiful woman like you are. You're so beautiful I sometimes forget to breathe when you're around."

Jamie swooned. I made gagging noises. "Come on, Jamie, you're better than this."

I shook my head in disgust, but there's no stopping a woman who's fallen for the wrong guy. "I need to do a final inspection. I'll leave you two to whatever this is. Fancy, come on, girl." I whistled and she came trotting to me, Lulu trailing along behind.

As I pushed my way past Luke and back inside I told myself I should be grateful Luke had taken such an interest in the store. Without him we would've never recovered from the fire in time to meet our grand opening date. But I wasn't so sure the tradeoff of having him around was worth it.

I found Katie in the café's kitchen, her nose pressed to the glass as she watched Luke and Jamie.

"He isn't worth it, you know."

She flinched back and pretended to be wiping down the counter. "I don't know what you're talking about."

"Look, I was seventeen once, too. And when I was I thought it was so cool how these older men found me attractive. Like, wow. A man not a boy and he wants *me*. But I'll tell you something…You get to be that man's age and you think about being attracted to a seventeen-year-old and then you realize how downright skeevy that really is. Jamie and I grew up with Luke. He's old enough to be your father."

She threw the washrag in the sink. "I said I don't know what you're talking about. Just leave me alone, would you?" She stomped past me. "Tell Jamie I had to go, but I'll be here tomorrow."

She strode across the seating area and yanked the front door open, setting all the bells along the top jangling. I had to lunge for Lulu's collar to keep her from following Katie outside. Did the girl have no sense for anyone but herself? Geez.

I muttered curses as I turned to inspect the store one last time, telling myself I had better things to do than try to protect one seventeen-year-old girl from getting her heart broken by a loser. That was just part and parcel of growing up—letting some guy sucker you into thinking he was more than he was. She'd learn.

Hopefully before she turned eighteen.

CHAPTER EIGHT

THE NEXT DAY DAWNED CLEAR AND BLUE AND PERFECT. Fancy and I left for a quick walk around the neighborhood —not up the mountain, one dead body was enough for us, thank you very much—as the sun was just starting to rise, coloring the sky all pink and orange.

I took a deep breath as I watched the colors spread along the horizon, reminding myself that no matter what happened from this moment onward at least I'd tried.

I could've easily stayed in DC and kept making good money while being silently miserable, but I hadn't. I'd taken the chance to get what I wanted. And even if I failed, even if I had to go back there some day to put a roof over my head, at least I'd know I'd tried. And the time I was getting with my grandpa—as long as I left his crosswords alone and kept him from shooting someone—was invaluable.

If I'd waited another ten years, it might've been too late. For all of it. It would've certainly been too late to spend quality time with Fancy.

As we reached the corner and passed by Luke's rundown house, I stuck my tongue out. You'd think for someone who billed himself out as a construction contractor that he'd make a little bit of effort to keep his house from looking like a derelict dump. But no.

When we'd been up on the mountainside the day before I'd been able to see into his backyard. It was a mess, full of rusted and rotted metal. I was surprised someone hadn't called him in as a health hazard yet. Maybe if he kept playing with Jamie the way he was, I would.

Serve him right.

As I glanced up the mountainside I saw Mr. Jackson headed towards the ridgeline, a pack on his back. Interesting. I hadn't figured he kept that path tended as a hobby. Maybe the extracurricular product that I'd spied down in the valley belonged to him.

Could he have killed Jack? A little drug dispute gone bad? Maybe Jack had tried to steal his product and he'd put an end to it the best way he knew how. He certainly knew his way around a gun—he always had extra deer or elk meat to offer the neighbors and had served in 'Nam. Maybe he was even trying to frame my grandpa by using a shotgun. He had seen that fight after all.

I pondered the thought as I walked along, liking it more and more as I thought it through. But then I shrugged it off. If Mr. Jackson had killed Jack, Officer Handsome would figure it out soon enough, he didn't strike me as the type to miss something so obvious. And, really, it wasn't my business. Let the cops handle it. I had a business to run.

Personally, I didn't care if they ever caught the killer. I

was just glad Jack Dunner wasn't going to be around to bark at me and my dog anymore.

About half a block later I saw Katie running towards me on the other side of the street, her long red ponytail swinging back and forth with every step, headphones snaking up to her ears, her arms moving with such perfect precision I wondered for a split second if she was actually a robot.

I waved, but she didn't so much as flinch, even though she had to have seen me. Not a ton of people out that early after all.

I entertained myself the rest of the walk around town trying to figure out what career Katie would excel at. Fashion CEO a la *The Devil Wears Prada?* CIA operative tasked with seducing Russian oligarchs? Prison warden? Nah, a prison warden would need to be friendlier than that. Maybe headmistress of a military school. That had possibilities.

I know. It wasn't very nice of me—I told you before I'm a horrible person—but I just don't understand people who don't like dogs. I mean, it was bad enough when she snubbed Fancy that first day—broke her little heart—but Katie didn't even like Lulu. Who doesn't like a golden retriever puppy? And even more than that, who takes a job at a *dog barkery* if they don't like *dogs?*

I didn't get it. Any of it.

Ah well. She was a hard worker at least.

When she was there. She certainly needed to duck out early quite a lot. But now that we were opening that was going to stop or she was going to find somewhere new to work. Jamie would object—she's nice that way—but eventually she'd see that you can't run a business if no one's there to serve the customers.

With that cheery reminder, I headed back home to change and get to the store. It was show time.

I was so scared I was trembling as I pulled up outside. I knew the café side would do well—people need their coffee and cinnamon rolls—but it was the barkery side I worried about. It wasn't exactly a small-town concept, so I'd be relying on tourists to find and like it. Not the easiest audience to court. A loyal customer is gold that keeps paying day after day, but I'd be trying to run a business based on drawing in new customers week after week. Not the best strategy.

At least we'd planned for all outcomes. If the barkery did fail, we'd just expand the café into the barkery side and I could still bring Fancy to work.

It just wouldn't be the same, that's all. Plus, I don't like to fail. It's not me.

Fancy cried in my ear, reminding me that we couldn't sit in the car all day, we had to get inside and get open. Jamie was already there—probably had been since four or five—baking up all her daily goodies. I was lucky enough that all the dog treats could be made a day or two before, so I got to "sleep in" as much as Fancy ever allowed me to.

(You should know that as much as I make little comments here or there about Fancy, that I adore her more than the world. So don't for one minute think that I don't happily roll out of bed at an ungodly hour and schedule my entire day around my dog with anything less than absolute gratitude that I have her in my life. Truth be told, if it weren't for Jamie and my grandpa I could honestly say that I like Fancy more than anyone in the world. But that crying to get out of the car thing? Pure misery.)

I led Fancy inside, flipped on the lights on my side of the store, let her out the back to run around in the dog run with Lulu, and then snuck across to see how Jamie was doing. She was elbow-deep in dough and I could see what looked like muffins baking in the nearest oven. A tray of cinnamon rolls was cooling on a tall rack nearby, the scent heavenly.

"You need me to do some taste testing?" I asked. "First day of business and all. We don't want to put out an inferior product."

She laughed. "I set one aside for you. Right there. Have at it."

I took a bite and sighed in pleasure. It was still warm, the frosting all soft and gooey, melting on my tongue in that perfect way good cinnamon rolls have, the cinnamon blending with the sugar in a perfect ratio of spicy and sweet.

I would've been best friends with Jamie even if she couldn't cook, but it certainly didn't hurt things that she was magic when it came to baking. "I'm going to get so fat working here."

"Haha. Hardly. You know all the running around we've been doing getting this place ready? Just wait until we're open."

"I hope you're right." I polished off the last of the cinnamon roll and stared out the back window where I could see trees swaying in a slight breeze as Lulu and Fancy rolled around on the grass. "Do you think we did the right thing, coming back to the valley and opening this store?"

"Yes. Without a doubt. And, remember, I'm the one who grew up here so I had no illusions about it being some idyllic mountain paradise."

I threw a hand towel at her. "It is an idyllic mountain paradise."

"You keep telling yourself that, Ms. I Found a Dead Body." She threw the towel back at me with a laugh. "Something doesn't have to be perfect to be worthwhile, you know."

I narrowed my eyes. "Are you talking about Luke?"

"And what if I am?"

"He's a player, Jamie. You have to see that."

"Just because a man flirts doesn't make him a player. He makes me laugh. You should be glad I'm getting out there again."

I sighed. Jamie had been through a really ugly breakup six months ago and I'd worried about her. She's a person who isn't happy outside of a relationship. (Unlike me. Give me a good book and I'm just fine all alone, thank you very much.)

"Promise me two things," I said.

"What's that?"

"One, you won't fall for him. You'll keep in mind what I've told you about him and assume that he is probably flirting up half the county."

She pursed her lips, but nodded. "Okay, fine. And two?"

"Two, you'll keep an open mind about other men and try to find someone a little more worth your time."

She grimaced.

"Jamie, please." I heard the front door jangle and glanced out front to see Katie walking towards us. I turned back to Jamie. "Promise? That you'll look for someone better than Luke?"

She shrugged one shoulder.

"Promise?"

"Promise."

I grinned at Katie as she joined us. "And you can help, Katie."

"Help with what?" She glanced at us, emotionless as always.

"Help me find Jamie someone better to like than Lucas Dean."

Katie stared at me like a deer caught in headlights.

"Maggie! You are not going to start enlisting people to find me someone better to like. If someone comes along, fine. Until then, I am just fine with Luke, thank you very much. Katie, can you get started putting out the fruit cups? I hadn't had a chance to do that yet."

"Sure." Katie pushed past me towards the big walk-in, her steps stiff and robotic.

Resisting the urge to check her neck for an off switch, I left them to their prep work. I'd have enough time later to keep working on Jamie. I just wanted to see my best friend happy, that's all.

CHAPTER NINE

THE WEEKEND WENT BY IN A WHIRL. WE'D PLANNED THE grand opening to coincide with a big dog show that was being held in the resort event center nearby so we'd had non-stop customers in both the barkery and the café from when we opened on Friday all the way through Monday.

It was great. And exhausting. So I was very happy to have my day off on Tuesday. We'd agreed when we opened the store that as much as it might be good for the business for us to both work seven days a week that that just wasn't sustainable. No point in opening your dream store and burning out in the first six months.

We wanted to love what we were doing, not hate it. And anyone who tells you that when you really love something it isn't work hasn't had to be on their feet for ten hours straight while keeping a smile on their face under all circumstances.

So Tuesday morning—after a nice walk around the neighborhood where I saw Katie doing her running thing once more, but no sign of Mr. Jackson hiking up the mountain—I settled down in the backyard for a little peace and quiet. At least I knew I wasn't going to have some weird man barking at me or Fancy this time.

(I know. A man was dead. I should be more respectful. But he barked at me. I mean, really. How torn up was I supposed to be over a man like that?)

We stayed out there until the sun was high enough in the sky to take away all the good shade spots. I love that space, but there are no trees, so after about 10 am it's not a pleasant place to sit. Walking back into the house, I heard my grandpa talking softly and paused by the laundry room, wondering if he was so far gone already that he was talking to himself.

I crept forward, trying to figure out what he was saying—to see just how crazy he'd become—when a woman's laughter rang out. I let out the breath I'd been holding and walked down the rest of the hall towards the kitchen.

A woman I didn't recognize was sitting at the kitchen table with my grandpa. She was well put together, her white hair tied back in a bun, her clothes neatly pressed and tidy, earrings on her ears, rings on her fingers (lots of rings), and bright red lipstick. I looked her up and down with a touch of disapproval. My grandparents had been married forty years and would've stayed married forever if my grandma hadn't died. I wasn't sure I liked the thought of some well-put-together woman honing in on my vulnerable widower of a grandpa.

I stepped forward. "Hi. I'm Maggie. Lou's granddaughter. Who are you?"

It's possible I was a little forceful with my question,

because she laughed. "I'm Lesley Pope. But we've met before."

"When?"

"At the library. Your grandparents used to bring you in when you were visiting. Always had a book in hand. Some things never change." She nodded towards the book I was currently holding.

I'll admit that hearing that she was or had been a librarian made me soften towards her. Just a bit, though. She was still honing in on my grandma's turf.

"Are you still a librarian? Don't you need to get to work?" I set my book down on the table so I could cross my arms as I glared down at her.

"Maggie May. You leave Lesley alone. I had friends before you decided to become my live-in nursemaid, and if I have to choose between those friends and having you stay here, I'll choose them. So scoot along now."

I looked back and forth between them. "Is that all you are? Friends?"

"Maggie May. I am eighty-two-years-old. My mother has been gone a long, long time and I don't need you stepping up to take her place. Now if you don't mind?" He nodded towards the living room.

"Fine. Nice to meet you Lesley." I stomped away, noting that he hadn't actually answered my question.

"And you, Maggie," Lesley called after me. She actually meant it, too.

I didn't. I was too busy wondering if she was taking advantage of my poor, bereaved grandfather.

As I walked across the living room I heard her say, "24

Down is INGRATE. I-N-G-R-A-T-E." My grandpa thanked her, his voice soft and warm.

So *she* could help with his crosswords, could she? Harrumph.

I couldn't figure out what to do with myself while she was there. Lock myself away in my bedroom like I was twelve? Sit in the living room and pretend I couldn't hear them talking softly in the kitchen? I'd already taken Fancy for her walk, and I was forbidden to set foot in the barkery on my day off.

Fortunately, she didn't stay for much longer. I wandered into the kitchen to make Fancy's lunch and casually said, "Lesley seems nice" as I wet and microwaved Fancy's food for her.

"Mmhm. She is." My grandpa didn't even look up from his paper. Stubborn old man.

"How do you know her?" I asked, leaning against the counter in as unassuming a pose as I could manage.

He chuckled. "Maggie May."

"Maggie."

"*Maggie.* I have lived in this town for forty-one years. I know everyone who lives in Creek who's over the age of twenty."

I set Fancy's food in her bowl and turned to look at him. "You loved Grandma."

"I did."

"But…"

He leaned his elbows on the table. "But your grandma is

gone. And I've been alone. And it's nice to have an attractive woman who knows crosswords to talk to on occasion. She also plays a mean game of Scrabble if you're ever up for it."

I frowned. "Do you think…I mean, would you ever…I don't know, get married again?"

He shook his head. "Lesley's already married."

"What? Grandpa!"

"It's not like that, Maggie. We enjoy each other's company and her husband…well, he's…he's not well. He's still at home, but he needs a lot of care. And sometimes Lesley just needs to get away from it all for a bit. So she comes here and we talk. That's all we do. Talk. And I'd appreciate it if you kept that to yourself. No one else knows and no one needs to know."

"I'm sorry. I'm just worried about you, that's all. I don't want her taking advantage of you when you're vulnerable."

He snorted. "I've never been vulnerable a day in my life. You should worry more about yourself and less about me. What did you think of Matt? He's grown into a good man despite some hard times. Found himself in the military. It's good to see."

I gave Fancy her after-lunch treat and sat down across from him. "I have big plans, Grandpa. And they don't involve falling in love. Not now. Maybe not ever."

He pressed his lips together and looked at me for a long, long moment. "I'm sorry to hear that, Maggie. I can't imagine what my life would've been like without your grandma. I hope you find what we had someday. And I hope when you do, you don't let it pass you by because of those plans of yours."

I grimaced. Just like he didn't want to have to explain

Lesley to me, I didn't want to have to explain all my twisted feelings around what he'd just said to him. "Love you, Grandpa. You up for a game of Scrabble? Or you only play when Lesley's around?"

"I think I have time for a game or two. But you better be prepared to be beat. I don't lose, even when my opponents are pretty."

I laughed. "That sounds like a challenge. And I'll have you know I don't lose even when my opponents are old and crafty."

CHAPTER TEN

I'D JUST PLAYED A SEVEN-LETTER WORD ON A TRIPLE WORD
score when someone banged on the front door loud enough
to send Fancy into a barking frenzy. "You get the door, I'll
shoo Fancy outside," I told my grandpa and ran to herd her
out the back.

She doesn't wear a collar at home and is too big to grab
and move, but I can usually step in front of her until I get
her going in the right direction. Plus, a good treat or two
works wonders once she's calmed down enough to realize
what I'm holding.

So while Fancy and I did the treat and two-step shuffle
out the back door, my grandpa answered the front door.
"Matt, good to see you again. You got my gun?"

I could just barely hear them from the laundry room as I
blocked Fancy outside.

"I'm afraid it has to be Office Barnes today, Mr.
Carver."

Hearing that, I ran back to the front of the house as

Fancy howled in protest—I almost never lock her out alone —but I couldn't worry about her right then.

"Why? And who's this?" my grandpa demanded as I slid around the corner and ran through the kitchen.

"This is Officer Clark. He's here to…well, to help me if you decide not to cooperate."

"Cooperate? That's all I've done so far. What's this about, Matt?" My grandpa was almost shouting.

I put a hand on his elbow to calm him down, silently hoping he'd let me step in before he said something he shouldn't. "Officer Barnes. If you could just explain what's going on, I think we'd both really appreciate it."

Matt nodded, lips pressed tight. This wasn't the warm man I'd met the other day, but someone doing a duty he didn't like. "Ballistics on the gun came back. It was the one used to kill Jack Dunner. And all the prints we could find on it came back to you, sir."

"Well it's my gun, ain't it? It should have my prints. That all you're going on?"

Officer Clark moved his tobacco around in his mouth as he leaned forward. "There's also the fact that you're a known killer. Did it before, why wouldn't you do it again."

"That doesn't count."

I stared at my grandpa. "What's he talking about? I thought you'd done time for robbing banks not murder."

"It wasn't murder, it was manslaughter. And if I hadn't shot the man he would've shot his wife and who knew who else. If I had it to do all over again, I would, but that doesn't mean I killed Jack Dunner."

"Grandpa," I muttered. "You're not helping things."

He held my gaze. "Maggie May, I've done a lot wrong in

my life, but the one thing I haven't done is lied to people about who I was or why I did it. Was robbing those banks a mistake? Yes, it was. But when you're young and poor it's hard to see other paths you can take. I broke the law and I did my time, but I ain't never been a liar and I ain't going to start being one now. That man I shot was like a rabid dog and he needed to be put down. If I hadn't done it, he'da hurt a lot of people that day."

He turned back to the officers. "I'm telling you, Matt, I didn't do this."

Matt nodded. "I hear what you're saying, sir. I do. But I need you to come in for questioning. You're not under arrest. Not...yet. And hopefully we can clear all this right up and you can be home in just an hour or two. But I do have to take you in. This is my job, sir. Somedays I don't like to do it, but it has to be done."

My grandpa thought about it for a long moment and then nodded. "Fine. Let me get my hat."

"I'll come with you," I said. Fancy could handle herself for an hour or two just fine.

Matt stopped me. "Sorry, Maggie, but you might as well stay here. You won't be allowed into the interrogation room with him."

"Should I call him a lawyer?"

My grandpa came back, settling a stained old ballcap with a John Deere logo onto his head. "I don't need no lawyer, Maggie. We'll sit down, we'll talk this through, and we'll get it all cleared up in no time. You just stay here and enjoy your day off."

He gave me a kiss on the cheek before stepping out the door, Officer Clark following after, his hand on his gun like he really believed my grandpa was going to make a run for it.

I looked at Matt. "Should I call him a lawyer?"

He shrugged one shoulder. "I hope it doesn't come to that. If...If we end up arresting him, I'll let you know. And if we're gone more than two hours, swing by the station, that'll mean we weren't able to clear things up easily."

"Okay. Thank you."

I watched him walk down the path and slide into the driver's seat of his police cruiser, my grandpa seated in the back like a common criminal.

Only after they'd pulled away did I step back into the house. I had a lot to think about. Not the least of which was the fact that my grandpa had actually killed someone and I'd never even known about it.

I texted Jamie to ask how busy the store was, desperate to tell her what had happened and get her advice, but she didn't even text me back for ten minutes and when she did it was a one-word text.

Slammed.

So I paced the house, tried to read my book, watched some horrible reality dating show that made me cringe so much I finally had to turn it off, and then paced some more. I finally got so desperate I started cleaning. I dusted all the bookshelves in the front room, washed all the dishes that were in the sink even though I could've just thrown them in the dishwasher, and even mopped the kitchen floor.

When my grandpa still wasn't back after all that, I

turned my attention to poor Fancy. "You know who could use a bath," I told her.

She immediately ran out the back door and to the far corner of the yard, staring back at me with those big sad eyes of hers like I'd just committed the ultimate betrayal by even mentioning the b word.

"Come on now. You know you could use one." I approached her with a handful of treats, hoping to lure her inside.

She took the treats, but stayed right where she was.

"Fancy…Look at your paws. Don't you think you'd like to wash that dirt off?"

When it comes to baths, logic doesn't really work with Fancy, but persistence does. I kept at her until she finally ducked her head and slunk into the house. When she was younger I'd had to herd her through the house, closing one door at a time until we finally reached the tub, but now she just resigns herself to her fate and goes straight to the bathroom like she's going to her execution.

What's crazy is she'll happily splash around in even the smallest of puddles but call it a bath and she suddenly hates water.

I closed the bathroom door—just to be safe, we didn't need her running through the house shaking water all over everything—and started the water running.

Fancy buried her face against my chest in sheer misery as I soaked her down and soaped her up. At least she didn't fight me. I'm not sure what I'd do if she ever did. Probably just let her be very, very dirty for the rest of her life.

It was all over in ten minutes. I toweled Fancy down as best I could—not easy with a dog that has a double coat like hers—and then let her loose. Looking at how black the water that drained out of the tub was I knew she'd definitely needed it.

Now you'd think that a dog that hates baths as much as she does would immediately flee once the bath was over. Not Fancy. She'll run out of the bathroom shaking herself all over anything she can find, but then she'll come back and hang around while I'm cleaning up. I'm not sure what she's thinking when she does that, but she does it every single time.

Crazy girl, but I love her.

Anyway. When I'd finished wiping down the tub—I get a lot of hair off of her during a bath—and went out to the kitchen for a Coke I found my grandpa at the kitchen table working on a crossword puzzle like nothing had happened.

"You're back," I said, sitting down across from him.

"I am."

"Did they clear you? Is it okay?"

He shook his head. His hand trembled as he tried to fill in his crossword. I reached out to put my hand on his forearm where his *Born to Lose* tattoo was, the faded green snake wrapped around a dagger a reminder that his life hadn't always been coaching baseball and going to church in a small town.

"So what happened? What did they say? What now?"

He set the pen down. "They said Jack was probably killed sometime the afternoon of the sixteenth."

"The day after I arrived then. So the same day you threatened him."

He nodded.

"While I was at the store with Jamie."

He shrugged. "That's what it looks like."

"What did you do after I left that day?"

He reached for his non-existent cigarettes and cussed, slapping the table in frustration. "I'll tell you what I didn't do. I didn't track that man up the side of a mountain and gun him down with my shotgun."

"Grandpa. I wasn't saying you had. Was Lesley here that day?"

"You're not bringing her into this, Maggie May."

I was too going to bring her into it if they arrested him, but for the time being I let it go. "So what now?"

"Matt said they don't have enough to arrest me just yet, but that I should stick around town."

"Do they have any other suspects?"

"I don't know. Why should they keep looking? It was my gun and the man was shot behind my house. I suspect it's only a matter of time before they make it official."

"Grandpa, if Lesley was here you have to tell them."

He shoved away from the table. "No, I don't."

"But you could go to jail."

He stared out the kitchen window for a long moment. "I've done time before, I can do it again."

"Grandpa! You're eighty-two-years-old, you can't go to prison."

But he wasn't listening. He'd already turned his back and headed to his room. Stubborn old man. I glared after him for a long moment before making up my mind. If he wasn't going to give the police his alibi, then I was.

CHAPTER ELEVEN

THE LIBRARY WAS AT THE EDGE OF TOWN IN A SHINY NEW brick and glass building that didn't really fit the rest of the town. When I was little the library had been housed in two connected rooms at the top corner of the courthouse, books crammed into every nook and cranny from floor to ceiling, the smell of stone dust and books hanging in the air.

I'd loved that place. The intimacy of being surrounded on all sides by books had called to my soul even if the lighting was horrid and actually moving around those two rooms had posed a significant health hazard.

The new place was fine. It had a large central area with comfy couches, four computers along the wall that anyone could use, two large meeting rooms, and a series of individual study rooms as well. I wasn't sure the actual book collection was any bigger than it had been, but I'm sure the airy space appealed to...someone. Just not me.

Lesley, who'd been manning the check-out desk, saw me as soon as I arrived. "A big change, isn't it?"

"Yeah. It's definitely different."

She laughed, the deep smile lines on her face showing that she'd always been a happy woman. "I miss the old place, too. It was my own personal hideaway—just me and the books stashed away in those little rooms. I read every book in there at least once."

"Really?"

She shrugged, laughing softly again. "Really. Can't say I'd ever want to re-read the book on the different makes of Chevy vehicles through the years, but I wanted to know what we had in our collection for when someone needed a book on a specific subject. And you'd be surprised how often that particular book was needed."

I couldn't help but match her smile even though it felt unfair to my grandma's memory. Darn Lesley Pope for being so nice and likable.

I glanced around. There was one little girl at the computer; her mother was seated in the corner flipping through a magazine, but paying more attention to us than whatever was on the page in front of her.

"Do you think we could talk? Privately?"

Lesley pursed her lips but nodded. "Give me a minute." She went to the back and returned trailing a young man with pock marks all over his cheeks. "Ron, Maggie. Maggie, Ron. Ron's the new librarian. Took over after I retired. Maggie used to visit her grandparents each summer and was one of my best customers when she was around. We're just going to catch up, but if you need me, knock."

"Alright, Ms. Pope."

We chose the meeting room farthest from the bored

mother. As we stepped inside I told Lesley, "The first library book I ever remember reading was *A Wrinkle in Time*. Were you the one that recommended it to me?"

"I am. I thought you'd like the main character. And for more than just a similar name."

I chuckled. "You know, I made people call me Meg for the next six months after I read that book. Until a couple of boys at school started calling me Meg the Hag, that is."

"Kids can be cruel."

I settled into a seat while Lesley closed the door.

"Eh. A few well-placed kicks and they stopped. Too bad I have to resort to words and reason these days…"

Lesley laughed as she sat down across from me, but then her face stilled and she looked right at me. "Are you here to tell me to leave your grandfather alone?"

The chair squeaked under me as I lurched forward. "No. Oh, gosh. You probably don't even know yet."

"Know what?"

"After you left, the police came by and took Grandpa in for questioning. The gun that killed Jack Dunner was his. And his are the only prints they could find on it. Also, I wasn't home at the time they think Jack was shot, so Grandpa's their prime suspect since he doesn't have an alibi." I watched her carefully as I added, "Not to mention, he's killed a man before."

Lesley didn't even flinch at my mention of how Grandpa had killed before. "Oh, poor Lou. He's worked so hard to put his past in the past."

"So you knew about that? About him killing someone?"

She looked at me with a twinkle in her eye. "You kids are

so funny. You all think that your grandparents have always been the way they were and never stop to think that they had a whole lifetime they lived before you ever came along. Of course, I knew about it. It was my sister's husband he shot."

"Really?" I leaned forward. "Was he…a bad man like my grandpa said he was?"

She nodded, the color leaching away from her face. "He was. Beat my sister every time he got drunk, which was at least two or three times a week. But she wouldn't leave him. Not until she had her son and he went after the boy. Finally she saw some sense. That night she waited until he passed out, packed up whatever she could find, and came to me."

She ran her fingers along the edge of the table, not looking at me as she continued. "Lou and I were seeing each other at the time. He said she could stay with us and he'd protect her until things blew over."

"Wait? You and my grandpa dated?" I'd known my grandparents hadn't gotten together until my grandpa was out of prison and already in his forties, but it had never occurred to me my grandpa could've dated someone else before he met my grandma.

"We did." She smiled looking back at the past. "We'd been together about ten months when this all happened. Were talking marriage but hadn't made it there yet. And never did, because two nights after my sister came to stay with us, her husband showed up with a gun."

I gripped the edge of the table, trying to picture it.

"There were about eight of us there at the time— including your grandma and her boyfriend, Gene. My sister's husband kicked in the door, screaming about how he was going to kill my sister and anyone who kept him from her, and pointed his gun right at me." Her hands started to shake so she clasped them tight together and held them in her lap. Her smile was gone. "I refused to tell him where she was, so he cocked the gun."

She met my gaze. "That's when your grandfather shot him. Saved my life that day. Probably saved my sister's, too."

I sat there, stunned. How had I never known this story? What else didn't I know about my grandparents? Or my parents for that matter.

She twisted her wedding ring around and around as she continued. "I told your grandfather I'd wait for him to get out of prison, but he wasn't having it. He told me that he loved me more than anyone in the world but he wanted me to be happy and he'd understand if I moved on." She glanced at the ring and shook her head. "I didn't want to. I loved him. I held out for two years, but then I met, Bill, my husband, and there was something special there. Something worth pursuing."

She looked me in the eye. "Still is. I love my husband to this day. Bill and I got married a few months later and then, the day after I found out I was pregnant with my first child, your grandfather found out he was being released from prison five years early due to overcrowding."

"Ooh." I winced, thinking what that must've been like for her. To wait for the man she loved, finally give up on him and move on, and then, just when it's too late to turn back, find out he was free. "Was this before the armed robberies then?"

She nodded. "Yes. Your grandfather moved in with Gene after he was released, but Gene had taken up with some bad folks by then and…Well, I'm not sure your grandfather cared much about anything at that point."

"Wait. Is this the same Gene my grandma was dating when that man got shot?"

She laughed. "Of course. Gene was your grandfather's brother. Didn't you know that he'd dated Marie before he was killed in that robbery?"

"I'd never heard his name before. My grandpa doesn't talk about these things much."

"He's worked hard to put it all behind him." She twisted her wedding ring around and studied the small diamond in a simple setting for a long moment. "He was out for less than a year before he was arrested for those robberies. By the time he was released the second time, Gene was dead and Lou had nowhere to go. My husband hired him on at the mine, Lou started spending time with your grandma, they fell in love, and the rest is history."

"Wow. How did I not know any of this?" I shook my head, trying to make sense of all the crazy connections I'd never known about. "My grandpa said your husband's sick?"

She folded her hands in her lap and looked at me, sorrow shining in her eyes. "He's in the final stages of Parkinson's. I care for him as best I can, but it's not easy. Sometimes I just need a break from it all and that's what your grandfather gives me." She held my gaze. "I love my husband, Maggie. And I will stay with him and stay faithful to him until the end. But I love your grandfather, too. Always have, always will."

I didn't know what to say to that. It wasn't at all what I'd expected to hear, but I suspected that if I asked my grandpa his feelings on the matter he might say he loved her, too, which was something I wasn't quite ready to think about.

So I changed the subject. "Do you always go to my grandpa's before you volunteer at the library?"

She nodded. "Every Tuesday and Wednesday."

"Which means you saw my grandpa the day after I arrived. The day Jack Dunner died."

"I did. I wasn't planning on it, but he called after you headed out to the store, so I dropped by for lunch and a quick game of Scrabble."

"You can tell the police. Give him an alibi."

She laid her hands flat on the table. "It won't help, Maggie. I was only there an hour. He had the entire afternoon to still shoot Jack. And…" She held my gaze. "Think of all the pain it would cause if people found out about Lou and me."

"But you said you just talk. That there's nothing more to it."

"We do. But do you think the town gossips will believe that? Do you think that, given my history with Lou and how sick my husband is that they'll really believe that all we do is talk? Do you think they'll ever let it drop? We'll be ten years in our graves and they'll still be talking about how I seduced poor old Lou while my husband was at home dying."

I bit my lip. She was right. I knew she was. Even though I hadn't grown up here, I'd heard enough over the years. In a small town it's almost impossible to escape who people think you are, no matter what proof you give them.

I drummed my fingers on the tabletop. "Do you think he did it?"

"No. Of course, not."

"Are you sure? I mean, he did point that shotgun at him."

She reached across the table and took my hand. "Maggie, your grandfather did not shoot Jack Dunner. He told me what had happened that morning, but he was laughing about it. He wasn't angry."

There was a part of me that wanted nothing more than to drag her straight to the police station so she could tell Matt and clear my grandpa's name. But she didn't deserve what would happen next. Neither did my grandpa.

Which meant I had to find another way to clear him. I had to find the real killer.

"Okay." I stood up, needing fresh air and movement, needing to think.

Lesley didn't move. She was still sitting there, turning her wedding ring around and around on her finger.

"Thank you," I mumbled. "For...for being there for him now that my grandma is gone. I think...He needs that. So I'm...I'm glad he has you." It was hard for me to say, but it needed to be said.

She dabbed at her eyes with a small monogrammed handkerchief and then stood up and straightened her clothes and hair, looking impeccable once more. "Thank you for that. I appreciate it. And I hope we get the chance to know one another better, Maggie."

"Me too."

She left without looking back.

I took a moment to get myself together, wondering

where to now. I couldn't clear my grandpa by providing his alibi, so now I had to find the killer. But who could it be? Who would've wanted Jack Dunner dead so bad that they'd follow him up a mountainside and shoot him? And who would know about my grandpa's gun? And the argument they'd had that day?

I didn't know, but I was determined to find out.

CHAPTER TWELVE

DECIDING TO SOLVE A MURDER AND ACTUALLY DOING SO are two completely different things when you're not a cop. You know how they say that determination and hard work can overcome any obstacle? Yeah, they're lying.

Good access to information, others who know what you don't, and the authority to investigate where you're not really wanted are much more helpful. All determination will get you is frustration when you refuse to quit. But it's all I had.

So I figured if I didn't have the information and authority, I'd go to the man who did. Officer Handsome. Matt.

The police station was only a few blocks away. As I walked there, I enjoyed the crisp spring air and tried to let my thoughts cool down a bit. I cut across the parking lot towards the single-story yellow sandstone building that housed the jail and main police station for the county.

It wasn't very impressive inside. It was newly-built, but small, with a central reception desk and four desks behind that, two on each side of the room, facing one another. Behind those were two offices with glass panes that faced the reception area, each holding one more desk. I assumed somewhere down the hallway were the interrogation rooms and jail.

This building was officially the main location for police in the county, but most of the time officers were out on patrol or at the auxiliary office in Bakerstown, so I guess they didn't need a big space. Like I said, Creek wasn't exactly a hotbed of criminal activity. Most of the time the cops were just dealing with out-of-town speeders or the same handful of drunks and domestics week after week.

Matt was the only one there, seated at one of the desks on the left. "Hey, Maggie." He waved me over.

I sat down across from him. "How bad is it?"

He studied me for a long moment, clearly trying to make a decision.

I waited, knowing that most people have a need to fill silence and that the more he said the more I'd be able to help my grandpa.

He rubbed at his chin where some late afternoon stubble had appeared. "You know, after my mom and I moved to Bakerstown I got into a lot of trouble. I was headed down a real bad path. Even landed in jail a couple times. Finally, my parents gave up on talking sense into me and my dad dragged me over to your grandpa's house. Seems your grandpa had sat him down when he was younger and out of control and helped him turn things around."

"I could see him doing that."

"Yeah, he's good that way. Your grandpa gave me some hard truths that day. Made me realize I didn't want to end up in jail or dead before I was thirty. So I enlisted. I needed the discipline and to get out of here for a while. Sometimes you don't appreciate what you have until you lose it."

That hit a little too close to home for me, but I shoved the thought aside. I was here about my grandpa, not to remember my own mistakes and hurts, so I just nodded. And waited, hoping he'd get to the point soon before someone walked in.

He sighed and rubbed at his chin again. "Which is all to say, I owe your grandpa. But I don't know how to help him. Ben—Officer Clark—is so fixated on your grandpa for this that he's not even willing to consider other suspects."

"Maybe I can help."

"How?"

I jerked back in offense and he held out a hand to calm me. "I'm sorry, Maggie. I'm not saying you can't help, I just…How?"

"Let me see what you have. Maybe there's something there you missed."

"Are you a trained detective? A forensics expert?"

I counted to five, not wanting to say the first thing that came to mind. When I felt calm enough, I said, "No. But I'm someone else who wants to see the real killer caught as much as you do. And since Officer Clark doesn't, you should be grateful for any other set of eyes. Even those of a rank amateur whose only exposure to law enforcement has been watching the Justice Channel."

I couldn't help but add that last bit. He was right. I'm not a trained detective or forensics expert. But I am smart. And observant. And, most importantly, I cared enough to keep pursuing this to the end.

"Okay." Matt opened a folder on his desk and turned it towards me. "This is what we have. Your grandpa and Jack had a disagreement the morning of the sixteenth. Your grandpa threatened to shoot him. The weapon used was your grandpa's, and the only prints on the weapon are his."

Before I could argue all the reasons that didn't mean my grandpa had shot Jack Dunner, Matt raised his hand and added, "But…Your grandpa could've shot Jack when they had that disagreement and he didn't. That makes it far less likely that your grandpa tracked him down later and shot him. Only your grandpa's prints were on the gun, but there weren't fingerprints on the barrel or the trigger, which means somebody probably wiped the gun down after using it. Also, the gun was stored in an unlocked location where anyone who knew about it could've found it and used it. We also found various shoe and boot prints along the trail, none of which matched your grandpa's shoe size."

"Okay. So you could argue it either way." I nodded, thinking. "Would it help to know that my grandpa spoke to someone else that day and told them about what had happened with Jack and that he was laughing and not angry when he did so?"

"Yes. Absolutely. Who was it?"

"I can't tell you."

"Maggie…" He leaned forward, fixing me with an intense blue gaze that made my thoughts skitter.

I shook my head. "I can't. I promised. But suffice it to say that he talked to someone about it later that day and that he was not the least bit angry."

"He could've already shot him by then."

"No. This would've been before that."

Matt narrowed his eyes at me, but I refused to let him rattle me.

I leaned forward, resting my elbows on the desk. "Okay, then. So we throw in this conversation with this other person and it's clear it wasn't my grandpa. Who else could it be? Do you have any other suspects?"

He shook his head. "Plenty of people hated Dunner—you saw what he could be like. But I haven't found anyone who hated him enough to kill him."

"Any signs he was caught up in drugs?"

"He definitely used them. But on a larger scale? Not that I found. I could ask around, see if he was making any moves in that direction. Why?"

It sounded silly now that I was about to say it out loud, but it was the only lead we had. "Well…I was thinking that maybe Mr. Jackson shot him. Over drugs."

"Your neighbor, Mr. Jackson? The old man with the raspberry bushes? Why would he shoot Jack Dunner?" He closed the folder and pushed it aside, not even reaching for a pen.

"First, he knows how to use a gun, right? He served in 'Nam and hunts regularly, even off-season. So we know he's willing to break rules he doesn't agree with."

"Hunting deer is not the same as killing someone."

"I know. I'm just saying. Also, the day I arrived, I saw him maintaining that path. He was up there trimming back tree branches to keep it clear, so there's something up that way that matters to him. Another day when I was out walking Fancy in the early morning I saw him headed up the trail with a pack."

"Okay. So the man likes to hike in the mountains and

keeps a trail clear so it's easier to do so. Doesn't make him a murderer."

"He should've found the body before I did, though, if he uses that path regularly."

Matt thought about it, but shook his head. "Still not seeing it."

"Also, someone's growing something down in the valley behind Harm's Ridge. If it's Mr. Jackson and what he's growing is illegal and Jack Dunner found out about it and tried to steal it…"

He grimaced. "Then that might be motive for murder. But that's a lot of ifs."

"It has to at least be worth investigating, right? I mean, Mr. Jackson also knew about the argument. And I assume he knew about the gun."

"True. He's really the only other person who knew about the argument, isn't he? Hm." Matt rubbed at his neck, thinking. "Well, it is better than what I have right now, which is nothing. I guess I could check it out."

"Can I come with you?"

Just then Officer Clark came in through the front door, slurping from a McDonald's cup. He tossed a bag that smelled of grease onto Matt's desk and glared me down until I stood up and stepped out of his way. The seat groaned under his weight as he sat down.

"Interviewing a witness without me, Matt?"

"Nah. Maggie and I go way back. We were just getting caught up." He opened the bag and laid out a Big Mac and fries in the middle of the desk. "Thanks for this, man. I owe you."

"Yeah, sure, no problem."

I looked at Matt's pathetic excuse for a dinner and shook my head. "Is that how you eat all the time?"

"Not a lot of fast food options around here, you know."

"You could cook."

Matt laughed. "You don't want to see me try to cook. I can burn water."

I bit my lip. Which was more important to me? Keeping my distance from Officer Handsome or saving my grandpa from jail time?

"How about you come around for dinner tomorrow night? We can finish catching up and you can have at least one meal that isn't a heart attack in a sack."

"Really?" He grinned at me, his eyes twinkling. I instantly regretted inviting him over. But done was done.

"Really. Six o'clock. Don't be late. My grandpa's a stickler for timeliness."

I left before I could change my mind, but that twinkle in Matt's eyes followed me all the way home.

CHAPTER THIRTEEN

BY THE TIME I CLOSED UP SHOP AND DROVE HOME THE next night I was already regretting my dinner invite to Officer Handsome. I could've just called the station to see what he'd found, but no, I had to go invite Mr. Distraction to dinner. I swear, sometimes I'm my own worst enemy.

My grandpa made it worse when he insisted that I set the table in the dining room. And not with normal plates, but with my grandma's china instead. And wine glasses. I stared in shock as he set a bottle of merlot on the table.

"Wine? China? You do know it's just Matt coming over for dinner, right?"

"Company is company, Maggie May. You think your grandma would've let us have guests over and sit on the couches with TV trays?"

"Well, no. But…"

"Just because she's gone does not mean I'm going to devolve into some sort of savage."

I shook my head as I finished setting the table.

"Grandpa, Matt's probably used to living on MREs and eating off of dirt floors. And I'm not talking about his time in Iraq either."

"All the same."

I continued to grumble as my grandpa sliced up the roast from the slow cooker while I whipped up gravy to go over the top and put the vegetables into a separate serving bowl. The last thing I needed was for Officer Handsome to go getting any sort of *ideas*.

When Matt arrived he was freshly showered and smelled like some sort of very pleasant cologne. He also had a small bouquet of flowers in his hand that my grandpa insisted I place in a vase and put on the table. I studied both of them, but from what I could tell they'd each come up with their part of things independently.

Still. I wasn't going to let this sort of thing continue. China and wine and flowers…What was this? Didn't they realize we had a murder to solve?

"So, what did you find out? Was Dunner getting into dealing drugs? Is that what someone's growing in the valley? What did Mr. Jackson have to say?"

My grandpa leaned out of the kitchen. "Maggie May, that is no way to treat a dinner guest. You want to talk business, you can wait until after the meal. Talk about something else."

That meant small talk. I hate small talk.

Matt and I stood there awkwardly, staring around for something, anything to say that wasn't connected to the investigation.

"So, Iraq…" I said at the same time he said, "I can't

believe that's still here," and gestured to where I'd scrawled his name on the wall all those years ago.

Since he'd knelt down to run a finger over the shaky letters, I was stuck with his chosen line of conversation. I knelt down next to him. "My grandpa claims nothing will take it off. I suspect he just likes to leave it there so he can tease me about it."

"He teases you about it still? How?"

I had to look away before I drowned in those blue eyes of his. "Every single time I start dating someone new, he makes a joke about hiding the permanent markers. Or asks me if I scrawled the guy's name on my walls yet. Every. Single. Time."

My grandpa came out of the kitchen, Fancy trailing along at his side, her nose in the air to smell the roast. "That's why Maggie's stopped telling me when she starts dating someone new."

"No, I've just stopped dating, thank you very much." Before either of them could pursue that one further, I stepped into the kitchen and grabbed a plate for Fancy. As I took my seat, I set the plate on the floor next to me.

My grandpa glared at me, but I chose to ignore him. We might have guests, but too bad, Fancy deserved to be a part of the meal, too. Matt looked at the plate on the floor and then back at me. "Dare I ask what that's for?"

"It's a sharing plate. For Fancy."

"A sharing plate." I could see him struggling to keep a straight face, but I ignored him as Fancy settled down next to me, her paws on either side of the plate, a thin line of drool falling from her left jowl in anticipation of the yummy meal to come.

"Yes, Maggie May. Why don't you explain to our guest what a sharing plate is." My grandpa eyed me from across the table, but I chose to ignore him, too.

"It's very simple. I like to feed Fancy scraps when I eat, and I don't want to just throw the food on the floor, that would be messy. Or get my fingers all slobbery, either. So I set down a plate for her. Simple as that."

I placed a small piece of roast on Fancy's plate. She gobbled it up and immediately looked to me for more, silent and waiting.

Matt smirked. "You set down a plate for your dog? At every meal?"

"Every meal." My grandpa nodded, his face grim, as he served himself vegetables.

Matt and my grandpa both tried to keep straight faces but failed miserably.

"You know, there are reasons I like living alone. Like not having someone sit there and judge me all day every day."

"You're welcome to live alone if you want to, Maggie May," my grandpa said as he covered his roast and vegetables with a thick layer of gravy followed by a healthy amount of ketchup.

"But then I couldn't help you out, Grandpa."

"Like I said."

I dropped a piece of carrot onto Fancy's plate and then served myself as my grandpa proceeded to tell Matt how I'd decided I needed to move in with him because he was so old and helpless. Except, somehow when my grandpa said it, it sounded like the most absurd idea in the world.

I glared across the table at him. "Need I remind you that

the first day I was here you pulled a shotgun on someone and are now the prime suspect in that man's murder?"

He shoved a potato in his mouth and chewed, glaring right back at me. "Need I remind you that that happened even though you were standing right there?"

Matt held up his wine glass. "A toast."

We both glared at him.

"To old friends," he lifted the glass in my direction, "men of wisdom", he lifted the glass in my grandpa's direction, "lovable balls of fur that eat off plates like dainty old ladies", he nodded to Fancy, "and a meal that isn't a heart attack in a sack."

"Cheers." I clinked glasses with Matt and my grandpa and let the conversation drift towards less weighted topics, trying not to think about how easily Matt had managed to charm both Fancy and my grandpa.

And me.

CHAPTER FOURTEEN

AFTER DINNER MY GRANDPA PULLED OUT THE SCRABBLE board.

"I thought we were going to talk about the case now," I muttered. That was the whole reason I'd invited Matt over after all, not...this.

He handed me the tile bag. "No reason we can't play and talk at the same time."

I sighed and drew an H. Matt drew an A and pumped his fist in victory. My grandpa drew a Z and handed the bag back to him to let him draw his tiles. "Competitive a bit?"

"There's nothing wrong with wanting to win." Matt laid out his tiles and handed my grandpa the bag next.

I laughed. "Oh, you're going to do well here. But don't think that because you drew that A that you'll actually win. We're serious Scrabble players in this family."

"Bring it on." He grinned at me and I couldn't help but grin right back.

We settled into an intense, but fun game of Scrabble.

Matt tended towards longer words and trying to hit as many double-letter or triple-letter scores as he could while my grandpa focused on making multiple words in one play. Me, I just held in there and tried whatever I could that would earn me enough points to keep up with them.

As we played, Matt updated us on the case. He'd checked out the valley, but it was a bust for now. The cabin was still there, but the plants were gone. Whoever had been using the valley wasn't anymore. Whether that was Mr. Jackson and he'd become spooked by the police investigation or whether it was someone else, Matt couldn't say. And without a good reason to do so he couldn't order the lab techs in to take fingerprints or soil samples. A county like ours didn't have unlimited resources.

He'd also swung by Mr. Jackson's house to talk to him, but Mr. Jackson wasn't answering his phone or his door.

"You know," my grandpa said. "I haven't seen Roy in a couple days. We don't talk much, but usually I see him out back or up the hill at least once a day. Didn't think much of it before, but if you couldn't get ahold of him…"

"Does he have any family around here?" I asked.

"No. He has a daughter back east, but they only talk on major holidays. I have her number somewhere around here. Let me see if I can find it."

While my grandpa searched through his old address book, I traded in all my tiles. I hate when I have only vowels to play. My grandpa wrote down the number of Roy Jackson's daughter—it was a New York zip code—while Matt played off a triple word score. I might've called him a bad word for that, but let's just pretend I didn't.

My grandpa chuckled as he counted up Matt's points. "Hm, Maggie. Looks like you've met your match."

I chose to ignore that little comment. "Maybe Mr. Jackson skipped town."

"What for?" My grandpa asked.

"Killing a man and getting caught growing illegal marijuana?"

Matt shook his head. "Too early for that. We hadn't even questioned him. As far as anyone else in this town is concerned, your grandpa is the killer."

"Thanks for that," my grandpa said.

Matt shrugged one shoulder. "It's true."

I sat back, thinking. "Fine, so Mr. Jackson is a dead end. Who else could've done it?"

Matt rearranged his tiles, studying the board intently. "I don't know. A lot of people didn't like Jack, but most felt the way your grandpa here did. That there was no point in wasting a bullet on a man who was going to find a bad end all on his own. He had no money for anyone to inherit. He had an ex-wife and two kids, but he stayed away from them and that's all they wanted from him. He probably had his hands in some petty crimes, but nothing I could find that was serious enough to warrant killing him. If you hadn't found that body, no one would've even cared that he was gone."

"Not even his mother?" I asked.

"Definitely not his mother."

I glanced over at Fancy who was asleep against the wall, snoring up a storm, and wished I could take back my moment of good citizenship. If I hadn't called the cops about the body, it would probably still be up there and my grandpa wouldn't be in danger of going to jail for a murder he hadn't committed.

Darned conscience.

I swore to myself that next time I found a dead body I was going to leave it right where it was. I needed to start keeping out of other people's business.

Yeah, like that was going to happen.

We wrapped up our Scrabble game and Matt left, no closer to finding the murderer than we'd been when he arrived. But I had to admit, it had been a fun night if nothing else. Wine, china, Officer Handsome, and all.

CHAPTER FIFTEEN

THE NEXT DAY WAS JAMIE'S DAY OFF AT THE STORE AND I didn't want to ask her to cancel it our first week of live operations, especially after she'd done most of the work getting the store up and running, so I dragged Fancy out of bed and we made it to the store by four o'clock to get started on all the café prep. As I sprinkled cinnamon on the dough for the cinnamon rolls I thought about how lucky I was that I only had to do this once a week.

I am not a morning person.

By the time Katie came in at seven I was ready for my first Coke of the day which would certainly not be my last.

(Don't judge. I don't drink coffee and I don't do crack, so if I want to have a Coke first thing in the morning and another one at noon and another one with dinner, then I think I should be allowed to do so without judgment. Sorry, but I'm a little sensitive around the issue given the number of people over the years who've told me about how you can dissolve a penny in Coke. The day I stop drinking Coke will probably be the day I get hit by a bus, so I'll enjoy my little addiction while I'm alive to do so, thank you very much.)

Anyway.

Katie and I made it through the morning rush without a single complaint about the food. Jamie *is* magic in the kitchen but I can hold my own, especially when I have her recipes to work with.

Katie and I were wiping down the tables on the barkery side when Lucas Dean walked in, grinning from ear to ear. "How are my beautiful ladies today?" he asked as he swaggered towards us.

I glared at him. "I realize it's probably a bit confusing for you, Luke, but the barkery is for canine dogs not human dogs."

"Haha. Funny." He gave Katie a kiss on the cheek and wink before turning towards me.

Katie blushed and gazed up at him, her eyes full of adoration. Seems my little "old guys wanting seventeen-year-olds is creepy" speech hadn't had much of an effect.

He took a step towards me and I twisted the dirty dish rag in my hand into a rope and held it out, ready to smack him if he came any closer.

"You wound me, Maggie. What can I do to convince you I'm a good man?"

"How about stop hitting on teenagers and leave my best friend alone? That'd be a good start."

He shook his head slightly. "Speaking of your best friend, she around?"

"No. It's her day off. Now, can I get you something or did you just come by to cause trouble?"

"As a matter of fact, if you still have any left, I'll take

one of those delicious cinnamon rolls of yours and a coffee to go."

I started to walk towards the café side, but Katie rushed past me, red ponytail swishing behind her. "I've got it."

"Probably for the best," Luke told me, watching her go. "This way I'll know no one spat in my coffee."

I stared him down. Spitting in his coffee was the least of the torments he deserved, the way he was playing Katie and Jamie and who knew who else. He pretended to ignore me, but I could tell by the way he fiddled with the salt and pepper shakers on the nearest table that he was well aware of my death stare.

Katie came back with the coffee and a to-go bag, staring up at him all gooey-eyed. He winked at her. "Thanks, doll."

"Make sure he pays with more than a kiss, please," I said, trying not to groan in disgust.

He handed over a bill I couldn't see and kissed Katie on the cheek. "Keep the change."

I mimed throwing up as he sauntered out the door in his tight jeans. Watching how Katie stared after him I wondered whether I could get away with permanently banning him from the store. That man was bad, bad news.

Unfortunately, I was pretty sure Jamie would never speak to me again if I did. Not to mention how much Katie might sulk. Broken-hearted teenagers are the worst.

The rest of the day was pretty uneventful. Matt stopped by right before we were supposed to close to tell me he still hadn't been able to reach Mr. Jackson and that his daughter didn't know where he was either.

When I got home I grilled my grandpa on who else in town might be capable of murder. He raised his eyebrows at the "who else" portion of that question, but we walked through a list of about five people he figured were capable of killing someone under the right circumstances, but then eliminated them just as fast for various reasons.

One would probably shoot any police officer who stepped foot on his property, but would otherwise keep to himself. Another would shoot anybody who crossed him in business, but Jack had stayed far away from him and for good reason. There was one woman on the list who would likely put any woman who came too close to her husband in the ground, but since Jack wasn't a sleazy young woman intent on seducing someone else's husband, we were able to eliminate her. And, of course, there was the man so gun-happy it was a miracle he hadn't shot himself yet, but he only used his guns on his home-built shooting range.

Crazy to realize how many people are probably capable of killing someone when you really stop to think about it, but none were the one we were looking for.

Frustrated and in need of some sign of progress, I snuck over to the Jackson house to see what I could see, but that was a bust, too. The shades were drawn, so I couldn't see inside. All I succeeded in doing was leaving footprints around the sides of the house.

I tried the back door—just in case, since my grandpa hadn't locked his front or back doors in forty years—but Mr. Jackson was a less trusting soul than my grandpa. The house was locked up tight. I wanted to try the front door, too, but didn't know how I could without someone seeing me and calling the cops.

I debated researching how to jimmy a lock online and getting in that way, but I decided that as much as I loved my grandpa I had to draw the line at committing a felony. He hadn't been arrested yet. If he ever was, then maybe I'd reconsider.

Disappointed in my progress, I trudged back home. It didn't help that things weren't going well at the barkery either. After that first big week with the dog show things had slowed down a ton, and I didn't feel like I was pulling my weight. Unfortunately, I wasn't sure what to do to fix things. I'd always known the locals weren't going to be my target customer, but I'd hoped the local business owners might chat us up to their customers a bit more than they were.

Frustrated by a lack of suspects, no Mr. Jackson, and disappointing barkery sales, I decided it was time to go on the offensive.

CHAPTER SIXTEEN

I SPENT MOST OF THE NEXT DAY IN THE BARKERY KITCHEN putting together sample treat bags. I couldn't use the Barkery Bites because they have to stay refrigerated, but I also make a great Peanut Butter Crunch Cookie that Fancy loves.

(Of course, Fancy loves anything that remotely looks like food, even bugs if they get too close to her out in the yard. She's not the most discerning of customers. Luckily for me, other dogs liked the cookies, too.)

So I cooked up a couple hundred cookies, bagged them up in cute little paw-print baggies with our logo on the side, tied them off with a 50% off coupon, and—as soon as the lunch rush was over—made the rounds of all the local businesses.

You would've thought I was running for mayor the way I shook hands and kissed puppies. I made sure to take time at each establishment—the resort, the local fishing guide's office, each of the fifteen restaurants in town, the five hotels, the three motels, the hunting lodge, the visitor's bureau, the rafting company, the realty company, and the two gas stations—to explain that I was new in town and that I'd just opened up a gourmet dog bakery.

I also just happened to let it slip that I'd been the one that found the body of Jack Dunner. I lost count of the number of times I said, "That was certainly a welcome to the valley I wasn't expecting." Fortunately, no one knew that my grandpa had threatened him with a shotgun the day he went missing—I'd have to thank Matt and Officer Clark for keeping quiet about that—but they all knew about Jack. Each and every one had a story about what a degenerate the man was.

By the time I finished my rounds I wasn't the least bit sad that he was dead. He'd lied, he'd cheated, he'd slept with other men's wives...But. Everyone also agreed that he'd never upset someone so much they would've bothered shooting him.

I pouted the whole way home. I'd spent an entire day baking, an entire afternoon schmoozing the locals, and I was no closer to finding who had actually killed Jack Dunner than I'd been the day before.

All I could hope was that my goodwill campaign would drive a little business my way.

The next morning I opened up the store and prayed that I'd have at least a few customers as a result of my efforts.

I did. But not the way I'd hoped...

By the next afternoon it was pretty clear that my efforts to make nice with the locals had worked, but that those efforts had had an unintended consequence I wasn't quite sure how to deal with. As I rang up an order of Doggie Delights I looked at the line of remaining customers and frowned.

First in line was Russell, owner of the local Big R and forty-year-old widower. He had a bit of a paunch but kind eyes.

Next was Dean, manager of the local resort and resident Lothario. Rumor had it he'd been making his way through every single woman between the age of twenty and fifty since arriving in town three months ago.

Behind him was James, one of the local fishing guides, originally from Australia. He was hilarious as could be but I was pretty sure he didn't even own a dog. He was also a bit short for my taste.

(Not to mention, I was busy operating a business, taking care of my grandpa, and tracking down a killer...)

After that was Martin, the sixty-year-old *married* man who ran the local specialty pizza restaurant.

Finally, at the very end of the line, were Evan and Abe, the only two I figured were legitimate customers. They owned the old historic Creek Inn and had a St. Bernard they'd named Lucy Carrots—Lucy for Abe's mom and carrots for the vegetable of the day the day they got her. No one had confirmed it for me, but I was pretty sure they had more of an interest in one another than they'd ever have in me.

I bit my lip as Russell leaned against the counter and

asked me to walk him through the display case selections the same way he had the day before. If he was flirting with me, he wasn't very good at it. He basically just grinned at me the whole time before finally pointing at the second-cheapest item in the display case with a soft grunt.

As I was ringing him up, Matt came in. He glanced down the line of men and smirked before going over to say hi to Fancy who'd jumped up and started wagging her tail the minute he walked in.

No sooner had the door closed than it opened again and Martin's wife, Gloria, stormed in. She marched right up to the front of the line and threw a bag of sample treats down on the counter. "How dare you," she cried.

"I'm sorry. What did I do?" I asked, genuinely perplexed. Did her dog have allergies? Did she not think I should be asking local businesses to help us promote our business? What had I done?

"Like you don't know. Going around town handing out your free goodies to every man in sight." She glared in the direction of her husband who turned bright red and took a step backward.

Matt managed to stifle his laugh. I wasn't so lucky.

I know I shouldn't have laughed at her—she really was genuinely upset with me—but if you could've seen the men lined up behind that counter...To think that I was trying to seduce any one of them was just absurd.

Her face turned almost purple and her eyes bulged out. I swear I thought she was going to collapse right there and then and that I'd have to call an ambulance and we'd forever more be known as the store where Gloria Parks had died of an aneurysm. "You...you...you temptress, you. How dare you laugh at me you...you *homewrecker.*"

I held my hands out to calm her. "Gloria, please. I'm sorry I laughed. I know this is very serious to you, but I'm not trying to tempt anyone with my..."

Matt leaned in. "With your *free goodies.* I believe that was the description she used." He was grinning from ear to ear.

I seriously wanted to slap him, but I was too busy trying to get Gloria to calm down enough to breathe.

Gloria gestured to the line of men, almost taking out Russell's eye in the process. "You think I'm going to believe you when I can see the proof of it before my very eyes? Look at them. Lured in here like flies to your honey trap."

It was all I could do not to laugh again, but I managed. Barely.

"Pick one," she demanded, waving her hand again.

"Excuse me?"

"Pick one."

"Pick one what?" I stared at the line of my customers as they all shuffled nervously and refused to make eye contact with me.

"Pick a man. I don't care who, but pick one. You pick a man and settle down and quit trying to cause trouble around here with your big city ways."

She stared at me like she actually expected me to just point at a man right then and there and settle myself down. Had she not noticed that her husband was one of my so-called choices? Or that the last two men in line had very likely picked one another already and had no interest in me?

I couldn't help but glance at Matt, but he was studiously looking at the ground not wanting to have any part of things now. (Figured the only man in the room I might want to pick was also the only man in the room who didn't want to be picked. Story of my life.)

I shook my head. "I'm sorry to disappoint you, Gloria, but I will not be picking a man today or any other day. I have my grandpa to see to and this business to run and I am not going to go off and settle down until those things are well under control. But I thank you for your concern."

I glanced to the side where Jamie had come to watch events unfold. "And I believe, Gloria, that if you go over to Jamie there that she'd be happy to give you one of her famous cinnamon rolls as a thank you for coming in here today. On the house."

I'm not sure that actually satisfied Gloria, but at that point her husband stepped forward and led her away. I let out a big sigh and turned back to Russell. "Sorry about that, Russell. That'll be $2.95."

All of my former admirers couldn't get out of there fast enough after that. At least they all bought something, even if it was the cheapest item available. Only Evan and Abe lingered to talk about the different products and what I thought Lucy Carrots might enjoy. They left with a whole assortment of treats, including a four-pack of the Doggie Delights.

Once the door closed behind the last of them, Matt stepped forward. "Maggie May, resident temptress who hands out her free goodies to every man she meets."

"Shut up. That was not funny."

He leaned his hip on the counter. "Maybe not for you. But it was certainly entertaining for me."

I straightened the counter even though it didn't really need it. "What are you doing here anyway? You don't have a dog, do you?"

"No, not yet. Someday, though." He scratched Fancy's ears as she shamelessly grumbled with pleasure.

I glared at her, but she didn't care. "So? Why are you here?"

The door opened and Darryl, a local hunting guide, came in. He saw Matt and frowned.

"How can I help you, Darryl?" I waved him forward.

"I was looking for more of those treats you dropped off by the office. Angus really liked them."

"Ah, perfect. Here. This should hold him over for a week or so. And half price since you're a new customer."

The way he kept glancing at Matt he was obviously another one who'd come by hoping for more than just dog treats to take home. I managed not to roll my eyes or acknowledge Matt's smirk as I rang him up and hustled him out the door.

"What did you do, hand out dog treats at the Creek Inn Friday night?"

"No. I just went around town handing out baggies of free dog treats at all the local businesses." I showed him the baggie Gloria had thrown at me. "I hoped it would prompt people to send tourists our way, not...this."

"Don't worry. Word that you only care about your work will spread like wildfire when they all meet up at the Inn tonight for drinks. Poor guys. I'm sure there'll be more than one drowning his sorrows."

I crossed my arms. "It's not just my work. It's also my grandpa. And the little matter of a dead body without a killer, although I wasn't going to tell them that. Plus, there's nothing wrong with wanting something more from life than to be someone's wife."

"Spoken like the big city girl you are." He winked to take the sting out of his words, but I wasn't having it. I glared him down until he leaned closer and added, "Look. You think I don't get the same pressures you do? Good-looking hometown boy back from military service and with a good job? I must be looking to settle down and start a family, right?" He shook his head. "All I'm trying to do is figure out if I can stay here long-term or not, but every time I turn around someone wants me to meet their daughter or niece or neighbor."

"Good-looking, huh?" I teased.

"Compared to the competition. Or so I'm told." He adjusted the gun belt at his waist, not meeting my eye. "I'm actually here on official business. Sort of."

"Why? What happened?"

"Mr. Jackson's daughter was worried about not being able to reach him after I called. They didn't talk often, but that was on her not him. He always returned her calls within a day. So when she couldn't get ahold of him, she got worried and flew out here."

"And? Did he split town? Do you think he's the one who murdered Jack?"

Matt shook his head. "Definitely not."

"How can you be sure?"

"Well, because odds are two people didn't suddenly snap at the same time and decide to kill someone."

"He's dead?" I glanced around to see if anyone had heard me, but Jamie had made herself scarce. Not surprising since she was as bad as Gloria when it came to wanting to see me settled down. "Where did you find him?"

"His daughter found him. In the kitchen. She had a spare key."

I winced, remembering how I'd tried to open the back door. At least I'd used my sleeve so I hadn't left any prints, but that might've wiped away someone else's prints...And I had left a bunch of muddy shoe prints all around the perimeter...

Looked like this was going to be another dog-peeing-on-a-dead-body moment.

"Was he shot, too?" I asked.

"No. Baseball bat. That's actually why I'm here." He glanced around. "We're going to have to take your grandpa in for questioning again. I wanted to tell you before we did because it would be a really good time for that alibi of his to come forward."

"Why do you have to question him again? It's not like my grandpa's the only one with a baseball bat in town."

He winced. "No. But he's the only one with a bat engraved with his name and 'Thanks for 25 Years of Service' on it."

I buried my face in my hands. "Let me guess. He kept his baseball bats in his unlocked truck, too?"

"That's what I'm assuming."

What was I going to do now? My grandpa wasn't just the suspect in one murder, he was the suspect in two. And I could see the rationale as clearly as anyone. That he killed

Jack out of anger and then Mr. Jackson because he'd seen something he shouldn't.

"This just keeps getting worse," I muttered.

"I know. I'll also need to talk to you at some point about the last time you saw Mr. Jackson. We're trying to figure out exactly when he might've been killed. It's been at least a few days."

"Okay. Yeah. Sure." I shook myself, trying to get my mind moving again. "Does my grandpa know? About Mr. Jackson? And the bat?"

Matt shrugged one shoulder. "A little hard to miss the coroner's van and the three police cars out front. But he doesn't know about the bat. And I'd appreciate it if you didn't tell him. Only reason I'm here instead of there is because I figured you'd have enough sense to call him a lawyer instead of letting him rely on the truth to save him."

"So he needs a lawyer now?"

"It'd be a good idea. Mason Maxwell is the best one in the county and he lives just outside of Creek. Here's his cell. If I drive slow enough you should be able to get ahold of him and get him to your grandpa's house before I get there."

I took the card he handed me, flipping it over and over as I thought through everything that had to happen now. I hated being powerless, but so much of this was out of my control.

Matt clearly wanted to leave, but he hesitated, looking back at me.

"Thank you. For everything," I told him.

"Anytime. I'll do what I can for him, Maggie. If it

weren't for your grandpa I probably wouldn't be alive today. And if I were, I'd probably be behind bars."

I nodded as he gave Fancy one last pat on the head and left. He really was a good man. And a good-looking one, too. How inconvenient.

CHAPTER SEVENTEEN

I CALLED THE LAWYER. HE WAS SHARP. I COULD TELL JUST from the three minutes we spent on the phone. No fluff, no dithering, just what happened, who's involved, where do I need to go, I'm on my way now, goodbye.

Then I called my grandpa. I'd promised Matt I wouldn't tell him anything about the details of the murder, but I figured he better know that a lawyer was headed to his house and why.

To say he was not happy with the fact that I'd called a lawyer is an understatement. He used a few words I'd never heard before—and I've heard quite a few colorful words over the years; my first job was at a skydiving center with a lot of sports jumpers from all over the world passing through. It was an interesting education in multi-lingual cusswords. Among other things.

I finally had to play the worried granddaughter card on him to get him to calm down and agree to let the man represent him. (First, though, I had to acknowledge—three

times—that after forty-plus years living in Creek it was absolutely ridiculous that anyone could believe my grandpa
capable of killing not just one man, but two.)

After that, I didn't know what to do with myself.

There was no point going home since my grandpa
would be at the jail with Matt and the lawyer. Fortunately,
things at the barkery picked up just enough that I couldn't
leave Jamie alone, so I tried to put thoughts of what was
happening back in Creek aside as I smiled and helped each
customer who came through the door.

Fancy knew something was off, though. She kept
standing up and crying at me until I finally had to put her
out back in the dog run. Poor girl. She was just trying to
help, but the crying got on my last nerve and I didn't want
to take my fear out on her.

(I felt so guilty I ended up sneaking her three Doggie
Delights before closing time finally rolled around.)

As soon as the clock struck four I locked the doors with a
firm thunk and turned to Jamie. "You have time for a beer?
It's been a day."

"Of course." She wiped down the counter on the café
side as she answered, never one to stop unless she had to.

"Don't 'of course' me. When you get going with a guy
you can sometimes disappear for months." I opened the
small fridge I kept for personal beverages and grabbed two
Wooly Boogers—sounds disgusting but they're a yummy nut
brown ale made by Grand Lake Brewing Company—and

headed out back, Jamie following along behind me with the bottle opener.

She opened the beers while I sat on the ground with Fancy for a minute and apologized for having to lock her outside. Fortunately, Fancy's idea of being mad at me involved barking a little lecture and then licking my face and stepping all over me until I'd petted her enough to show that I really was sorry.

After that was done I joined Jamie on the bench and took a long sip of my beer. I savored the taste as I looked at the tops of the trees swaying in a slight breeze, the mountains looming behind them on the horizon. As bad as things were, at least I had this moment, sitting outside after work with my best friend and my dog, a good beer in hand, surrounded by the beauty of the valley.

"I don't always disappear into relationships," Jamie finally said when it was clear I wasn't going to say anything.

"No? Tell me the last one where that didn't happen. Where you weren't practically living with the guy by the end of the first month of dating him."

She thought about it for a minute. "There was Neal."

"Neal? The guy from France that you dated for two weeks before he had to go back home?"

"Yeah. See, I didn't lose myself in a relationship with him." She took a sip of her beer as I shook my head.

"No, but you did talk about what it would be like to live in Paris. You even looked at one-way airfares, if I recall correctly. Probably would've gone if I hadn't pulled you back from the ledge."

Fancy came over and lay down so close her foot was touching mine. Poor girl. I really must've stressed her out.

She likes to stay close, but never that close. I rubbed her back for a second, listening to birds singing somewhere nearby.

Jamie elbowed me. "Speaking of men...Was that Matt Barnes I saw in the barkery today? Looks pretty good in a uniform if it was, but he just moved back to town from overseas. He doesn't own a dog, does he?"

I took a long swig of beer. Jamie and my grandpa should form a club. The Busybodies Club. "He was here on business." Because I wasn't quite ready to tell her what business, I added, "You know, he's single. And a helluva lot better man than Luke."

"Are you seriously trying to set me up with him?"

"Sure. Why not? He's good-looking, he's smart, he's kind, he's..."

"Yours."

I lurched to the side, scaring Fancy to her feet. "What?"

Fancy settled a few feet away with a huff of annoyance.

Jamie laughed. "Matt's been yours since we were kids."

"No he hasn't. We hardly know each other." I crossed my arms and glared at the mountains, thinking darkly about the disadvantages of living in a small town.

"You wrote his name on your wall when you were five."

"What does that have to do with anything?" I swore to myself I was going to go home as soon as I finished my beer and remove that name from the wall once and for all; I didn't care if I had to burn down my grandpa's house to make it happen.

"You used permanent marker."

"So? I was five. Do you think that was some sort of deliberate choice I made? Please."

Jamie laughed. "Do you know that my mom told me that when we were all babies. Not even talking yet, I mean, barely crawling. That our mothers put us all down to play and I crawled over to Matt and you crawled over there right away and shoved yourself between us? You couldn't even speak yet, but you'd already claimed him."

"And because *over thirty years ago*, when I was *a baby*, I pushed you out of the way, you won't go near him now? That's ridiculous. I've always hated girl dibs. You know that. He's yours if you want him. Go for him."

She laughed. "No point. He only has eyes for you, Maggie."

I choked on my beer. "Don't be absurd. There's nothing like that there. The only reason we're talking at all is because he has two murders to investigate. Plus, you know me. I don't do relationships well."

"That's because you've always been in love with Matt." She tapped her beer against mine. "And when you finally give up and acknowledge that fact I am not going to be the one standing between you."

She downed the last of her beer with a smug smile as I brooded. Rather than continue what had become a completely ridiculous conversation, I finally told her why Matt had been there that day.

"Oh your poor grandpa. At least you got Mason Maxwell to represent him. That man is amazing. I don't know why he lives up here and isn't dominating the courtrooms of some big city, but if anyone can get your grandpa out of this mess, it's Maxwell."

"He did seem pretty sharp when I talked to him, but if they don't have any other suspects I don't know what he can actually do. I mean, the bat and the gun were both my grandpa's. If it wasn't him, who hates him enough to frame him like that?"

"Didn't you say he had a secret lady friend? With a husband?"

"Who killed two men just to get back at my grandpa? Wouldn't it be easier to just shoot my grandpa instead? I mean, granted, the guy would've known about my grandpa doing prison time. But he's also really ill. I doubt he's physically capable of killing two people."

"So if your grandpa's not the target, then the two men who were killed were. What do they have in common?"

"Nothing except proximity to my grandpa. And maybe pot."

"Pot? That's legal now. Why bother killing someone over it?"

I told her everything I knew, because whether she wanted to admit it or not she had been a little caught up in Luke lately and we really hadn't had a chance to talk about any of this. But even after we'd talked through it we were no closer to finding a suspect to give the police.

As we sat there and watched the sun sink behind the mountains, Jamie asked, "Do you remember when we were little and they found that escaped criminal living in that cave up the mountain behind your grandpa's house?"

I nodded. Before the cops had found him, the local kids had. We'd snuck up to the cave and looked at the stacks of canned food and the dirty sleeping bag spread on the ground, daring one another to go inside until we heard a branch break in the woods somewhere nearby and ran away screaming.

"You think that's what it could be? Some weird survivalist living up in the woods who didn't want anyone to get too close? I mean, it's possible that whatever was being grown down in that valley wasn't pot after all. And that whoever was living down there in that cabin really didn't like being bothered by anyone…"

Jamie ran to grab us each another beer while I thought about it. If that's who it was, then there was really only one way to know…

She handed me a beer and the opener. "Don't you even think about it."

"About what?"

"About going to check that cave. If there really is some crazy psycho running around up there, the last thing you need to do is to cross paths with him. You're smarter than that."

I bit my lip. "He probably wouldn't shoot a woman. And he probably doesn't have his own weapons since the gun and the bat came from my grandpa's truck."

"You going to bet your life on that? And what if he decided to kidnap you instead of shoot you?"

I laughed. "Please. Last time some weird mountain man kidnapped a random girl in the forest was something like thirty years ago."

"That you know about. Just because they don't make TV movies about it anymore doesn't mean it doesn't happen."

I took a sip of my beer.

"Don't be stupid, Maggie."

"I'd have Fancy with me. She's like…a bear."

Jamie snorted as we both looked down at Fancy who'd

rolled over on her back and had her front two paws thrust into the sky as she snored away. "Yeah, somehow I can't picture the Fanster doing much more than licking the guy to death."

"She might bark at him first. Make him run away."

"What if he shot her instead? You don't want that."

I chewed on my thumbnail as I thought about it. As much as I hated to admit it, Jamie was right. But someone had to find this killer. And soon.

CHAPTER EIGHTEEN

MY GRANDPA STILL WASN'T HOME BY THE TIME I LEFT THE barkery and drove to Creek. It was weird to step into that dark, empty house. I'd never been there alone before. And it had never felt so cold and abandoned. There was a roast chicken going in the slow cooker, but I didn't know whether to go ahead and eat or to wait for him.

I was starving, but if he was going to be back soon then I'd wait. But the only way to know that was to call the jail and ask. And who was going to tell me the truth? Matt was probably interrogating my grandpa and no one else would have a reason to let me know anything about anything, especially if it was Officer Clark who answered.

I was just about to leave Fancy to walk down to the jail and see what I could see when the front door opened and my grandpa came in, muttering to himself as he disappeared down the hallway. He was followed by a man who was immaculately dressed in what I like to think of as country club casual—nicely pressed slacks and what was probably a very expensive cashmere sweater. He had salt and pepper hair and a fierce intelligence that evaluated me and Fancy in the space of a few seconds.

Fancy, who normally would've seen a new man in the doorway and gone over to say hi, stayed right where she was, frozen by the warning look he gave her.

"That's an impressive trick," I told him as I walked over, nodding towards where she watched him, still unmoving.

"You just have to show them who's the alpha. Dogs are pack animals."

I raised an eyebrow at that, but didn't say anything more about it. "You must be Mason Maxwell. I'm Maggie Carver. Nice to meet you."

"And you." His handshake was firm, almost aggressive, but not quite.

"Would you care to join us for dinner? I'm sure my grandpa's as starved as I am and there's a chicken ready in the slow cooker."

"You two go ahead and eat. I'll eat at home. But I would like to talk about a few items with you before I leave."

I studied him for a moment, trying to read what was going on behind that chiseled exterior, but I drew a blank. The man was completely unreadable. How odd.

My grandpa returned, still muttering to himself. "I'm hungry. Mason, you staying or going?" He walked right past us into the kitchen and started throwing down plates for all three of us. (Not the china, though. And not in the dining room, but at the small table in the kitchen.)

"He's not eating with us, Grandpa. But he did want to talk to us about a few things."

My grandpa grumbled to himself as he put back one of

the plates. "You going to at least let me give you something to drink?" he demanded. "I'm not much of a drinker anymore, but I've still got a nice bottle of scotch around here if you're interested."

I silently prayed that Maxwell would at least accept the scotch. I was afraid that if he said he was fine or that he just wanted a water that my grandpa would direct all the stress and anxiety of the day at the one person he probably needed most to help him make it through this mess.

But Maxwell must have sensed that, too, because he inclined his head towards my grandpa and said, "I'd like that very much. Thank you, Mr. Carver."

I finished getting the carrots, potatoes, and onions out of the slow cooker and into a serving bowl and then joined the men at the table. I was so famished I didn't even wait to start serving myself.

"So?" I finally asked after I'd taken a couple of bites and seen that my grandpa had served himself, too. "What happened?"

"What happened?" my grandpa muttered, glaring at Maxwell. "This friend of yours showed up at my house, told me to let him do all the talking, and then proceeded to remind me that I was supposed to let him do all the talking for the next two hours while the cops tried to ask me perfectly innocuous questions."

"There is nothing innocuous about being questioned in the matter of two separate murders, Mr. Carver." Maxwell took a slow sip of his scotch and tilted his head to the side, clearly pleasantly surprised by the taste.

"I didn't kill either of those men. And I would've liked to be able to tell the cops that."

"You already did for the first one, yes?"

"Yes."

"And yet you were still the first person they suspected when they found the second body."

My grandpa harrumphed at that and shoved more food into his mouth.

"So where do we go from here?" I asked, sneaking Fancy a piece of chicken under the table. I wasn't comfortable putting down a sharing plate with Mason Maxwell in the room.

"I don't know. If they'd had enough evidence they would've arrested your grandfather instead of just bringing him in for questioning. But from what I can see they're not looking at anyone else for this. So one more piece of evidence and they'll probably arrest him. But until they do that...We just have to wait."

"I didn't kill anyone." My grandpa slammed his hand down on the table, making our plates jump and Fancy run outside barking. "I told them that. They should believe me and find the real killer."

"Mr. Carver, I wish the justice system were as efficient as that. It's not. You should know that given your history."

My grandpa stabbed at a piece of chicken. "I shouldn't need a lawyer to defend myself for something I didn't do."

"When it comes to matters of the law, Mr. Carver, we can all use a lawyer. Take for example the sentence you served for killing that man. He was in your home, with a gun, about to shoot someone. If that isn't justified homicide, I don't know what is. If I had been your attorney, you wouldn't have done time for what you did. You saved the life of an innocent woman and I would've made sure the judge and the jury saw that. You relied on the truth to protect you. It didn't. So if you don't want to repeat the mistakes you made back then and end up back in prison when you don't deserve to be, you need to listen to me. Do not say anything to the cops. Officially or unofficially."

My grandpa glared at him, but Mason Maxwell stared right back. I watched the two men lock their wills and worried that something in the room was going to break from all the energy they were directing towards one another.

Finally, my grandpa bowed his head. "Fine. I won't speak to the cops, officially or unofficially."

Mason Maxwell turned to me. "Same goes for you, Ms. Carver."

"But Matt's the one who gave me the heads up about the cops coming to question my grandpa again. If I hadn't been speaking to the cops, and if he hadn't given me your number, my grandpa would've been all alone there today."

"It doesn't matter. They are not your friends right now."

"But Matt gave me your phone number."

"Still doesn't matter. Do you want your grandfather to go to jail?"

"No." I fought the urge to pout. How did this man make me feel like a little kid caught with her hand in the cookie jar?

"Then don't speak to the cops until this is over. Not even so much as a how do you do."

I pressed my lips together. I knew that he was giving us the best advice he could. It was what I would've probably told any stranger in the same situation. But...

Matt was on our side.

Maxwell tried his glare on me, but I just ignored him. I could still feel it burning into me, though.

"Ms. Carver?"

"I heard you." I stabbed at a carrot with my fork as I tried to figure out how I could save my grandpa if I couldn't work with Matt. I'd be flying blind. Maybe it was time to go back up that mountain and see what I could find. I seriously doubted there was actually a killer lurking up there. I mean, how likely was that?

Of course if there was, it would be a really stupid thing to do to go up there.

But this was my grandpa we were talking about. I had to do *something*. Something more than wait around for them to find enough evidence to arrest him.

CHAPTER NINETEEN

THE NEXT DAY AT THE STORE I WAS DISTRACTED, TRYING to figure out what to do. Jamie had told me not to go back up the mountain, and I knew Matt and my grandpa would both tell me the same.

And yet...

I was going to need to take some sort of risk if I wanted to save my grandpa.

Jamie and I talked about it that afternoon while Katie cleaned up after the lunch time rush. (On the café side we had a panini and soup option that was really popular with both the locals and the tourists. I'd also started putting some of the barkery packaged items on the café counter and those at least were selling well now that my local admiration society had disappeared.)

"You can't put yourself in danger, Maggie. If you think there's something to be found up that mountain, then let Matt be the one who does it. That's his job."

"But Mason Maxwell told me not to talk to him. Plus,

he's not going to take the time to look over every little inch for clues like I would. I mean, yes, he owes my grandpa for getting him on the right path, but he's still not family, you know?"

Jamie shook her head. "I'm telling you, it's a fool's errand to go back up that mountain."

"Do you honestly think there's some crazed killer hanging out on the mountain behind my house? Really?"

"No. But that doesn't mean there isn't one." She started to refill the napkin dispensers.

I joined in to help out, the clanging metal sound as I shoved napkins into each one suiting my mood. "Tomorrow's my one day off for the entire week. It's my only chance to find something to clear my grandpa's name. I'm out of options, Jamie. What else can I do?"

"I suppose relax in the backyard and read a good book isn't an option?"

"No."

"Maybe you should ask around to see who might've wanted to kill Mr. Jackson? You haven't done that yet, have you?"

As I considered the possibility, Lucas Dean strolled through the front door. (On the café side this time. Ever since my little comment about him being a dog he'd made sure to use the café-side door, which was just fine with me.)

I glared at him as he passed by Katie, just daring him to kiss her on the cheek like he had the last time he'd been in the store. If he did I was going to take all my pent up frustrations out on him and kick him out the door so fast his head spun. I was done with him and his hijinks.

But that's the thing about Luke. He's good at reading

women. So he didn't stop to kiss Katie on the cheek (although she did stare after him adoringly) and he also didn't kiss Jamie on the cheek when he reached us (although she also gazed at him like a love-struck teenager).

"Ladies. Is it too late for lunch?"

"Not at all," Jamie answered, smiling, even though I knew she'd already packed the leftover sandwiches up and stored away the soup in the walk-in. "What would you like?"

"You know what I like. Surprise me."

Jamie dimpled up at that while I rolled my eyes and resisted my childish urge to cough out a less than flattering description of him.

As Jamie went to the back to prepare his lunch, Luke turned so he was leaning with his elbows on the counter next to me, which allowed him to watch Katie who was wiping down the same table over and over again while glancing up at him every few seconds through lowered lashes.

I really hoped he'd do something horrible before that girl turned eighteen, because he was going to crush her like a bug when he got his hands on her.

To pull his attention away from Katie, I forced myself to talk to him. "How are you, Luke? What are you up to these days now that you're not working on the café?"

"This and that. Some fancy rich man's wife is moving in for a long stay in that mansion up on the hill, so I've been doing work for her. She has some interesting needs, including an entire room devoted to her Irish Wolfhound. You want to give me one of those little goodie bags of yours, I could leave it for her."

The last thing I wanted was to be indebted to Luke for anything, but business is business and if some rich socialite decided the barkery was worth patronizing that could turn everything around. So I gave him three of them. "For her and her friends."

"How generous." He leaned closer. "How come you can't be that generous with me, huh, Maggie? I remember you were much more generous when we were little."

I laughed. I couldn't help it. "Are you seriously referring to that one time we played 'show me yours I'll show you mine' from fifty feet away when we were, what, six or seven years old?"

"I'm just saying you used to be a little more open to adventure. Now you're...frigid."

If my grandpa hadn't already been under suspicion of murder, I might've taken Lucas Dean out for good right then and there. Frigid? Frigid? Because I didn't want to get involved with some cad who played on the emotions of every woman he met? Or because I had priorities in my life that didn't involve bedding the nearest man I could find?

Fortunately for Lucas I believed a family should only have one person under suspicion of murder at any given time.

Jamie returned with Luke's lunch and I took the opportunity to take Fancy and Lulu outside for a bit of play time. We all needed the diversion and I couldn't stand watching Katie and Jamie get all gooey over him for another moment.

Jamie joined me after Luke was gone. "Katie's watching the shop. You okay? What did Luke say to you that had you giving him the death stare?"

"It doesn't matter. I'm not wasting my breath on that man. I need to figure out what to do to help my grandpa."

I laughed as Lulu took a flying leap at Fancy, knocking her to the side. Fancy stared back at her as if asking, "What on earth was that about?"

Jamie laughed, too. "How about just spend some time with your grandpa tomorrow? If he does get arrested won't you want to have spent as much time with him as you could?"

"But if I can find out who really did this I'll get that much more time with him."

Fancy, not to be outdone by Lulu's acrobatics, took one large paw and pinned Lulu on the ground. Lulu squirmed free and ran to a safe distance before turning to bark at her.

"Leave it to the police, Maggie."

I pressed my lips together. I was never going to convince Jamie that my stepping in and trying to solve the murders was anything other than a foolish mistake that was probably going to get me hurt or killed. And sometimes the best way to keep a friendship going is to just agree to disagree without ever actually saying you've done so.

"Online sales have started to pick up," I said, changing the subject.

"Really?"

"Yeah. Maybe it's all the dog show folks ordering online to replace what their dogs have already eaten. I don't know. I'm just glad to see at least someone somewhere likes my barkery idea."

"Ah, Maggie. Success doesn't happen overnight."

Fancy came over to me and leaned against the side of the bench, keeping a wary eye on Lulu. I scratched behind Fancy's ears as Lulu grabbed her chew toy and started running around the yard, throwing it for herself. "Easy for you to say. The café's been humming along since day one."

"That's because people know what a café is. And if you give them good food at good prices, don't have too much competition, and have enough people with income in the area that can afford to eat out, you can succeed."

"Oh, is that all it takes?"

We both laughed because we were intimately familiar with all the statistics on how many restaurant businesses fail. Every single person we'd told about our plan trotted out some version of the number whether they knew what it actually was or not. The general consensus had been that we were doomed, doomed, doomed and would be crawling back to our old jobs within a year.

Jamie shook her head as Fancy decided it was time to take that chew toy from Lulu and raced after her, but Lulu easily kept head of her. "All I'm saying is that people need to get used to the idea of a barkery. And once you start drawing in the tourists you'll be fine. People who didn't bring their dog this time around will next time. And then you'll be turning customers away at the door."

"I hope not. Those poor dogs."

Jamie laughed.

After a second, I joined her. "If it isn't one problem, it's another, isn't it?"

Fancy gave up on chasing Lulu and collapsed into a heap on the grass. She only has about five minutes of good playtime in her at any given point in time. Lulu, fortunately, is about the same. She collapsed at Fancy's side.

"Ain't that the truth," Jamie answered me. "But I'd rather be so busy I had to take reservations than so dead I could sit outside here with you and the pups and not worry that Katie was going to get overwhelmed. Although it is pretty nice."

"That it is."

We both looked at the dogs, just in time to see Lulu open an eye and oh-so-casually scooch herself forward until she could chomp on Fancy's tail. Fancy shot to her feet with a yelp and turned to glare at Lulu who looked up at her, the picture of innocence, long strands of black hair hanging out of her mouth.

"I think that's my cue to take Fancy back inside before she decides to eat Lulu." I jumped to my feet and dragged Fancy away. I didn't really think she'd eat Lulu, but I wouldn't have put it past her to pin Lulu on her back and growl a very strong opinion about what could happen to puppies that bite other dogs' tails.

None of us needed to see that even if Lulu *had* earned it.

Meanwhile, Jamie went to remove the hair from Lulu's mouth and give her a small lecture about not biting Fancy. Given the tone of the words I was pretty sure it just sounded like praise to Lulu. That dog was going to be a hellion when she was full grown…

Unless I could tame her wild puppy ways first. As I led Fancy inside I brainstormed all the ways I could help with Lulu's training without Jamie noticing. What can I say? It's not in my nature to leave things be when I can do something about them.

Which brought me back to how to help my grandpa.

CHAPTER TWENTY

I TRIED TO TALK TO MY GRANDPA ABOUT EVERYTHING that night, but he didn't want to talk. He told me that he'd said his piece and now it was up to the law to figure out the truth of the situation and that there was nothing to be done until they did.

I brooded as we sat side-by-side on the couch and watched old episodes of *Frasier*. I wasn't in the mood for humor, not when a killer was on the loose and my grandpa was still the only real suspect. The only thing that kept me sane was playing Sliding Tiles on my laptop. Unfortunately, unlike the game—where if you slide all the pieces around enough you eventually get to the end—I couldn't see a way forward with the murder investigation unless I either risked my life or risked the anger of Mason Maxwell.

I didn't sleep well that night trying to figure out what to do next. I really, really wanted to go up that mountain. But I also knew that if there was actually something to be found up there that I'd be a fool to do so. One, because of the possible risk to my life. Two, because if there was forensic evidence then the cops should really be the ones to find and process it.

I was still law-abiding enough to think they were the best ones to find any evidence, although it was a close call.

When I took Fancy out for her walk the next morning she really wanted to go up the mountain. In her case, though, I knew it was because she'd found something smelly that one time and was hoping to find something equally smelly again. I resisted the urge to let her lead us with her nose and pulled her towards the street instead.

We passed Katie out for her normal morning run. She was as friendly as always—running past without even glancing our way. Weeks of working together and I still hadn't figured out what made that girl tick.

I decided to walk Fancy down to the ballpark and let her run around for a bit. It was a gorgeous morning and she'd earned it. Of course, her version of running around is to sink into the soft green grass of the ball field and watch the birds fly by.

Don't get me wrong, that's just fine with me. I knew a woman when I was in DC who had a Vizsla. She would run that dog a mile to the dog park, let it play for forty-five minutes, run it the mile back home, and that dog would still want to play more. I am far too lazy for a dog like that. Fancy fits me perfectly—one walk a day with the rest of the time spent sleeping or eating.

I sat down next to her and tried to enjoy the morning, but I just couldn't stop thinking about my grandpa and what I could do to save him. I looked towards the mountain where they'd found Jack Dunner's body—I couldn't see my grandpa's house from there, but I could see the ridgeline—but it was just a mountain like any of the other ten I could see from where I was sitting.

I wished I was up on my rock looking down on everything instead of down at the ballpark feeling lost, but I made the best of it by pulling out my phone and surfing Facebook to see what perfect lives people were pretending to have now. Like the friend who'd just posted all her photos of her amazing vacation in Mexico that I knew had involved spending three out of five days sick with Montezuma's Revenge.

I debated adding my own life-is-perfect photo, but I knew I couldn't do it. I'd add some silly caption like, "Gorgeous morning, too bad the cops still think my grandpa killed two men," and then I'd have to spend the rest of the day explaining and calming folks down.

Finally Fancy had had enough and we headed back. We passed Katie about a block and a half from home. I swear there wasn't a drop of sweat on her, which made me reconsider that robot hypothesis. I ticked all the clues off. Cold handshake, minimal smile, no acknowledgement of people she knew when she saw them on the street even though she lived in a small town, and now no sweating after what must've been at least a forty-five minute run.

At least her cheeks were a little flushed, but I bet a good roboticist could pull that off. Sweating, though? They probably weren't there yet. And women do sweat. I played sports in high school; I know. Or—for those ladies who claim not to do something as crass as sweating—women most definitely glisten. A lot.

Not Katie, though.

Muttering about the unfairness of life, I returned home, still not sure what I was going to do.

I finally settled for the sensible option. I called Matt at the station and reminded him that there was that robber's cave hidden away up the mountain and suggested that maybe if he checked there he'd find some additional clues about the murders.

He, of course, wanted to know if I had any specific reason for believing that the robber's cave held clues to the murders. I assured him that no, I did not have any specific reason for believing what I did and told him I would've been happy to investigate myself except for the danger of getting shot and all.

He laughed. "Oh, I see. You won't go check because of how dangerous it could be, but you're just fine with me getting shot?"

"No. I didn't say that. But as Jamie pointed out to me, that's *your* job, not mine."

"Is it now?"

I could almost picture him smiling on the other end of the phone and glared at the wall where I'd written his name all those years ago. I was not flirting, I swear.

"Alright," he said. "I'll check it out and then drop by after to let you know what I found."

"Um, maybe call. Grandpa's lawyer told me not to talk to you." I bit my thumbnail and turned away so I couldn't see his name anymore.

"And yet here you are...Just can't stay away..."

"Would you please just check out the cave and let me know what you found?"

"Yes, ma'am," he said, the laughter evident in his voice as he ended the call. Men. Can't live with 'em and you just can't shoot 'em.

That left me with nothing better to do but wait. I stationed myself in the backyard with Fancy and a book, but I wasn't really reading it. I was too busy watching for signs of Matt heading up the mountainside.

He and Officer Clark passed by around nine o'clock. Matt waved as Fancy ran up and down the fence barking at him, but Officer Clark didn't even look in our direction. I waved back and then settled in to wait for their return. But instead of either one coming back down the mountain, a police four-wheeler headed up the path about an hour later, an older woman behind the wheel.

I wanted to stay out there and see what happened next, but by then the sun was shining right down on me and Fancy was crying to be fed, so I reluctantly dragged myself inside. At least they'd found something. I just hoped it was the clue that would clear my grandpa's name.

CHAPTER TWENTY-ONE

THIRTY MINUTES LATER THERE WAS A BOOMING KNOCK AT our door, like a battering ram. When I ran to answer, hoping to see Matt standing there with a smile on his face, I instead found Officer Clark. He had on those mirrored sunglasses that wouldn't let me see his eyes, but his hands kept opening and closing like he wanted to hit something and his jaw was clenched tight.

"Where's Lou Carver?" he demanded, looming over me, his hand moving towards his gun.

"Why do you want him?" I asked, moving to block him from coming into our home. I know I should've been nicer, but the way he was acting scared me.

"None of your business. Is he here?"

I looked past him, hoping to see Matt coming up the drive, but it was just me and Officer Nasty in a showdown on my front porch. I was willing to poke the bear a little, but not enough to get arrested.

"Yes. He's here." I wanted to reach for my cellphone

which was stashed in the pocket of my sweatshirt, but I suspected he'd draw his gun on me if I did. I needed Mason Maxwell there to run interference before something bad happened.

Officer Clark put his hand on the door and moved towards me, but I held my ground, trembling with fear, but determined to keep him away from my grandpa until I knew what was going on. "I'm sorry, but I did not give you permission to enter my house. Why are you here? Do you have a warrant?"

I know. Stupid. But Fancy had started barking in the background and I didn't know what Officer Clark would do next. The last thing I wanted was for him to shoot her.

"Ma'am. I need to see Mr. Carver. Now." His voice lashed at me and I knew he was about a second from shoving me out of the way.

"Okay." I tried my best soothing the beast tone and held up my hands to calm him. "Let me just put the dog out back so she's not in the way and then I'll get him for you. Please wait here."

He clearly wasn't happy, but at least he took a step back instead of another step forward. I carefully closed the wooden door to a crack, wishing we had a screen door. The way Officer Clark was acting I wasn't sure what he'd do when I opened the door next. I wouldn't have been surprised to see him draw that gun of his.

First thing I did was block Fancy in the backyard. She did not want to go, but I wasn't going to risk her being shot. Second thing I did was call Mason Maxwell and tell him what was happening. He advised me to cooperate and keep calm and said he'd meet my grandpa at the jail. I wanted to ask why he thought they were going to take my grandpa in again, but given Office Clark's behavior it was pretty clear that's where things were headed.

I just didn't know why. What had they found in the old robber's cave?

Finally, I went to find my grandpa in his workroom at the back of the house. He was in the midst of assembling one of his miniature planes. It amazed me he could still do such fine work at his age. I chalked it up to stubbornness. I'd seen him take five minutes to attach one piece because his hand was shaking too badly to place it. Fortunately, he was just sitting there, staring off into space. I didn't think Officer Clark would wait five minutes.

"Grandpa. Officer Clark is here. He wants to see you. I think he's going to arrest you."

He nodded once, but didn't look at me.

"Grandpa?" I glanced towards the front of the house, sure Officer Clark was going to break down the door at any moment.

He wiped his hands on his jeans and reached for his non-existent pack of cigarettes. When he didn't find them he walked over to a locked cabinet in the corner, unlocked it, reached inside, and pulled out a fresh pack of cigarettes and a lighter.

"Grandpa! What are you doing?"

"If this is my last moment of freedom I'm going to smoke a cigarette by God." He started to unwrap the package but I stepped across the room and put my hand on his.

"Please don't do this, Grandpa. I know how hard it was for you to quit. And...Well, you won't have the same motivation to quit again this time. Don't let this set you back that way."

He glared at me, his hand shaking, tears in his eyes, before pulling his hand away and flinging the pack of cigarettes on the table. The only other time I'd seen him cry was when my grandma was dying. It shook me to my core to see him like this now.

He pushed past me and stomped down the hall towards where Officer Clark was waiting. I ran after him and stopped him before he could open the door, sure that if he flung it open the way I suspected he was going to that Officer Clark would shoot him.

"Let me, Grandpa. Officer Clark isn't in a good place right now. I don't know what they found up in that cave, but whatever it is, it's convinced him you must be the killer."

My grandpa stared me down and I shrunk back. "Maggie May, how do you know where they were looking this morning?"

I bit my lip, finally realizing what I'd done. "I told Matt to look there. I didn't know...I just...I thought maybe they'd find evidence of the real killer. I didn't know it would come back to you..."

His look was cold as ice as he stepped back and smoothed a hand over his hair. "Open the door, Maggie."

I grabbed the doorknob and slowly eased the door open, making sure to keep my body between Officer Clark and my grandpa.

"Here he is, Officer Clark," I said in my calmest voice even though I was trembling from head to toe.

Officer Clark focused on my grandpa, his body rigid with anger. "Lou Carver. You are under arrest for the murders of Jack Dunner and Roy Jackson. Please step out onto the porch. And keep your hands where I can see them." His hand dropped down to rest on his gun.

"He didn't do this. He's not a killer," I cried.

My grandpa stepped past me, slowly, calmly, staring off into the distance like a man walking to the gallows who knew there was no rescue in sight, his hands held up for Officer Clark to see.

"Grandpa!"

"Stay out of this, Maggie. You've done enough." He stepped onto the porch next to Officer Clark, never once looking back at me.

"He didn't do this," I cried again as Officer Clark wrenched my grandpa's hands behind his back. "Where's Matt?"

Officer Clark ignored me as he turned my grandpa and pushed him towards the squad car in our driveway.

"Does he know you did this?" I shouted.

But Officer Clark just kept on walking.

I dashed at the tears that filled my eyes as Officer Clark opened the back door of the car and pushed my grandpa inside, not treating him with the care you'd expect for an eighty-two-year-old man.

"I called his attorney," I shouted at him. "You speak to my grandpa before he arrives, I'll sue your asses to the end of time."

(Yes, I did use that language with that man. No, I'm not sorry about it. You see your grandpa put in cuffs and shoved into a squad car and tell me what you'd want to say to the person doing it.)

I turned my attention to my grandpa even though he probably couldn't hear me through the car window and still wasn't looking at me. "Grandpa, wait for your attorney. You do not speak to them until he's there, you hear me?"

Neither man acknowledged me as the cruiser backed out of our driveway and headed for the police station. I watched them go, my chest tight.

This did not look good. What had they found up there?

CHAPTER TWENTY-TWO

I didn't know what to do. I didn't know why they'd arrested my grandpa. I called the station and asked for Matt, but they said he wasn't in. I figured he must still be up the mountain with whatever they'd found there. But what was it?

Only one way to find out.

I threw on my hiking boots, leashed up Fancy, and headed up the mountain to confront the man who'd said he was on my grandpa's side but had just let him be arrested and was too coward to even be there when it happened.

I was full of righteous anger, rehearsing over and over again exactly what I was going to say to Mr. Matthew Allen Barnes, betrayer that he was. How dare he sit at my grandpa's table and tell us how much my grandpa had done for him and then turn around and do this? What kind of man does that? Certainly not the kind of man I'd thought he was.

Fancy wasn't too happy with me because I only let her

stop to smell things when I had to stop to catch my breath. Hiking at seven thousand feet is no joke. I finally had to slow down both for my sake and Fancy's. It's a good thing I have her around. She keeps me healthy in more ways than one.

I didn't want to. I didn't want to think. I just wanted to be angry and yell at someone, because I was scared. My grandpa didn't deserve this. He'd turned his life around. He'd been a vital part of this community for forty years.

But unless a miracle happened he was going to go back to spending his life in a cramped space with a bunch of dangerous men. At eighty-two-years-old. He couldn't do it. He'd die.

I pushed forward, scared and furious, my free hand clenching and unclenching, my calves aching, my lungs burning. Fancy kept looking at me, the worry clear in her eyes, but I couldn't calm myself, not even for her.

I found Matt outside the cave, flipping through a plastic file box full of folders. I could see the four-wheeler parked nearby and a woman I didn't know inside the cave taking pictures.

"How could you?" I shouted as soon as I was close enough for him to hear me

"Maggie! What are you doing? You shouldn't be here." He snapped the lid closed on the file box and stepped towards me, hands out to restrain me.

I glared him down. What did he think I was going to do? Make a mad dash for the stupid box and run away with it?

"How could you?" I screamed at him again, Fancy whining at my side.

"How could I what, Maggie? What are you talking about?"

Like he didn't know. I started to cry. I hate when I get angry and cry. I hate it. Which just makes me cry more. But I wanted so badly to hurt someone and I had no one to hurt. My grandpa had just been arrested and now Matt was standing there like he didn't know or didn't care?

"Don't pull that dumb act with me. You had him arrested. Officer Clark just dragged him away from our home in handcuffs."

Matt's first reaction was confusion, but that was quickly followed by a dawning realization of what must have happened, which was just as quickly replaced with an anger that matched my own. He pressed the button on his radio and said, "This is Officer Barnes. Get me Officer Clark. Now."

I crossed my arms, realizing I should've brought a coat with me. Even in early summer it can be chilly once you get into the higher elevations. I focused on taking deep breaths, trying to calm myself enough to make the tears go away. The area around the cave had an earthy, decayed smell that was almost but not quite unpleasant.

A woman replied over the radio, "Sorry, Officer Barnes, but Officer Clark is with a suspect. He said not to disturb him."

Matt swore and glanced back at the cave and the file box. "Sue, you okay if I take the four-wheeler for a bit?"

The woman in the cave nodded. "Yeah. Actually, if you take the boxes down with you, I can just walk back down on my own."

"Thanks." He strapped three boxes onto the back of the four-wheeler with bungie cords, his movements quick and efficient, those of a soldier in battle.

"What's going on, Matt?" I pulled Fancy closer when she tried to sniff at the boxes.

He jumped like he'd forgotten I was even there. "I can't tell you that, Maggie, I'm sorry."

He started to get on the four-wheeler and then turned back to me, his jaw tight as he flicked a glance at the woman in the cave. "There were photos, Maggie. Photos of your grandpa and Lesley Pope. Together."

"Together together? Or just sitting on the couch holding hands together?" Had Lesley lied to me? Were she and my grandpa having a full-blown affair?

"Sitting on the couch. Nothing...intimate. But for Officer Clark that was the motive he needed. I told him to wait. That your grandpa wasn't going anywhere. But..." He cussed. "I should've known. I don't know what his issue with your grandpa is, but he's had it in for him since day one."

He was standing so close I could smell his aftershave. "I'm sorry, Maggie. I'll do what I can, but it doesn't look good right now."

"Thank you." As he turned away, I glanced at the file boxes. Three of them. All of my grandpa and Lesley? "Wait."

Matt was already on the four-wheeler, ready to leave.

"Are those all of my grandpa and Lesley Pope?"

He shook his head. "There are photos in there of pretty much every single person in town. You were right about Mr. Jackson and the pot, by the way." He glanced at the boxes. "Anyone who thinks people in small towns don't cheat or lie should look through those boxes. But I gotta go, Maggie. Before Ben does something we all regret."

I pulled Fancy out of his way and watched as he drove down the mountainside. Now that my grandpa had been arrested and they'd found a motive for why he'd killed Jack Dunner, I wasn't sure what Matt *could* do. But I was glad he was still willing to try.

CHAPTER TWENTY-THREE

I COULDN'T GO HOME. I WAS TOO UPSET. SO I HEADED TO the big rock and sat cross-legged at the edge, looking down at the town I'd always thought of as a perfect haven from the real world.

How wrong I'd been. Creek was just like anywhere else in the world, a bubbling pot of conflicting needs and wants that occasionally boiled over into the worst sort of things people could do to one another.

What they'd found in the cave made a lot of sense. In our one brief meeting Jack Dunner had struck me as the type of man who wouldn't hesitate to blackmail his own mother if he thought there was profit in it. (Disagree if you want, but I think the fact that a man is willing to bark at a complete stranger shows a lot about his character and does in fact call into question his loyalty to his mother.)

I didn't want to believe my grandpa had killed Dunner. He'd told me he hadn't and I'd never had cause to doubt him before.

But...

It was his gun. And he had threatened the man. He had also made it quite clear he thought the world would be a better place without a man like Jack Dunner around. And he'd also made it more than clear to me that he'd do almost anything, including go back to prison, to protect Lesley Pope's reputation.

So which was I supposed to believe? The word of my grandpa, a man I'd know my entire life but not grown up around, who had had some tough times when he was younger, but who I'd never seen lie in over thirty years? Or the cold, hard evidence?

I tucked my knees up against my chest and rested my chin on them as I thought. Fancy looked up at me with those amber eyes of hers and cried softly.

I ran my fingers along one of her ears, letting the velvety feel of it calm and center me.

Gut or facts? Which to believe?

I stared at Fancy for a long moment and she stared right back at me, steady as the rock on which I was sitting.

Gut.

I didn't care what the evidence said. I knew *who* my grandpa was. And so did Fancy. He hadn't done this, which meant someone else had.

But who?

I didn't know. But I did know that it was time for my grandpa's alibi to come forward. No secret to protect there anymore. I needed to talk to Lesley Pope. Now.

I dragged Fancy home—poor girl was having a bad day between being locked out back, not being allowed to enjoy her walk up the mountainside, and then being dragged back home. Well, at least she hadn't been arrested and thrown into jail like my grandpa. It's never easy when you have to choose between those you love, but I knew she'd recover. She's a forgiving kind of girl.

She curled up on the goldenrod couch with a loud sigh while I rooted around for my grandpa's address book—I'd seen where he kept it when he gave Matt Mr. Jackson's daughter's number. Lesley's number was easy enough to find, the digits in my grandma's handwriting. I shoved the hurt of that to the side as I dialed her number.

"Hello? Lou?" she answered, clearly surprised to be receiving a call from my grandpa's number.

"Lesley, it's Maggie."

"Maggie, what's wrong? Is your grandfather okay?" I could hear the tension in her voice, but I wasn't sure if it was concern for my grandpa, worry that her husband would overhear her on the phone, or both.

I took a deep breath to keep from crying. "They arrested him for the murders."

"Oh no. When? Why? I thought they didn't have enough evidence?"

"This morning. Officer Clark came for him. He was so angry I thought he was going to shoot him. I don't know why that man has it in for my grandpa, but he does. Matt said he hasn't wanted to even consider another suspect ever since he heard my grandpa was involved."

Lesley sighed. "I know why."

"You do?"

"The past just won't stay in the past, will it? The man your grandfather shot was Ben's grandfather. Ben's father, Mark, was the man's son from his first marriage and Mark has always questioned whether he was really abusive like everyone said or whether your grandfather shot him for the money. My sister inherited fifty thousand when he died."

"So Officer Clark grew up believing my grandpa had murdered his in cold blood."

"Yes. And...My husband is Ben's mother's uncle, so he knows that my husband is sick." I could hear the tears in her voice. "Well, no reason to withhold that alibi now, is there?"

I spared a moment to feel sorry for this woman whose entire world was about to be destroyed. Because there was no way this was going to stay within the walls of the precinct if Officer Clark knew about her and my grandpa. By tomorrow everyone in town would know that my grandpa and Lesley were "close". Within a week that would be twisted by rumor into something more than just two people who cared for one another spending time together. This would haunt her—and my grandpa—the rest of her life.

I still loved Creek, but in that moment I really hated the way small towns can burn like wildfire with a juicy bit of gossip. I thought back to the three boxes full of photos and hoped there was something in there even more juicy than my grandpa and Lesley. Not that their lives would ever be the same after this, no matter what else the police found...

"Can I help?" I asked, not sure what to do now.

"No. Best if I handle this alone. Thank you for letting me know, Maggie. Hopefully your grandfather will be home to you soon."

I hoped so, too.

CHAPTER TWENTY-FOUR

I CALLED JAMIE NEXT—FORTUNATELY IT WAS LATE
afternoon by then and the store was slow—and told her
everything that had happened, including the fact that it was
my fault my grandpa had been arrested. Why had I thought
it made sense to tell Matt about the robber's cave before I
checked it myself?

"Don't be ridiculous, Maggie. You know you couldn't go
up there yourself, not with a murderer running around."

"But if I'd found the boxes…"

"What? What would you have done? Hidden the photos
of your grandpa and Lesley? You're not like that, Mags. You
might be able to not tell someone something you knew, but
you'd never destroy evidence."

I stared out the back window. She was right, but I didn't
want to hear it.

"I could've snooped through all the other photos and
found a suspect."

I sank down on the couch next to Fancy who gave me a

glare and hopped down to go sleep on her bed in the corner, her back to me. Great, I'd gotten my grandpa arrested and my dog was mad at me, too.

I had to fix this. Somehow.

"So what now?" Jamie asked.

"I don't know. Hopefully when they talk to Lesley they'll realize my grandpa didn't do this. But..." I bit my lip. The only way to be sure my grandpa wasn't going to be charged with murder was to find the real killer, which meant I needed time to investigate. I didn't trust that the cops were going to look for anyone else.

But Jamie was my friend and she'd risked everything to open this business with me. I couldn't bring myself to ask her for what I needed most. Fortunately, there's a reason Jamie's my best friend.

"Take tomorrow off. I'll cover for you," she said.

"Are you sure?" I protested while secretly thanking my lucky stars that she'd made the offer.

"Positive. You'll owe me one, though."

I wanted to hug her, but settled for, "Thank you, Jamie. You're the best."

"I am. And don't you forget it."

We both laughed.

"You have any idea who else could've done it?" she asked.

I shook my head, even though she couldn't see me. "No. But I bet the answer is in those boxes the cops found. Only question is, how am I going to get a peek at them?"

"Just remember, you won't be doing your grandpa any favors if you get arrested, too."

I shrugged that off. "I'm not going to get arrested. I'm just going to snoop around a bit, that's all."

"Maggie…"

"What?"

"Please be careful."

"I will. And thank you again for agreeing to watch the store." I hung up, the beginnings of a plan starting to form.

That plan solidified into something real when Morgan Maxwell called me half an hour later. "They're going to keep your grandfather overnight," he said, not beating around the bush.

"But he's an old man. He can't be in jail overnight." I thought of all the pills he took each day. He couldn't live without them. He was innocent but before I could prove it they were going to kill him with their stupidity.

"He's tough. He'll be fine. It's just a tactic to get him to break, but they don't understand that with a man like your grandfather the harder they push, the harder he'll fight them. I should be able to get him released tomorrow."

"Did they already question him? What did they say? What did they have? Is he still their only suspect?"

"They had some photos of him and Lesley Pope that Officer Clark thought meant something. The worst of the photos showed them sitting on the couch holding hands, though. I can't imagine a man committing two murders to keep it secret that he was holding a married woman's hand."

"Well, there is some history there." I told him what

Lesley had told me about their past and Officer Clark's grudge.

"Ah. I didn't know that part. Your grandfather isn't the most forthcoming client I've ever had. Thank you."

"Does it change things?"

"No."

"Did Lesley come by? Did she give her alibi for him?" Fancy had finally forgiven me and she came to sit next to me with a loud huff. She's not a fan of my being on the phone.

"She did, but it's not enough to change things at this point. Too much time that day of the first murder that's still unaccounted for. And with the photos, the police can allege she made it all up to protect him."

Fancy groaned and rolled onto her back demanding a belly rub. I tried to silently shush her, but wasn't very successful.

"So what now?" I asked.

I could almost see him shaking his head on the other end of the line. "Best thing that can happen now is the killer slips up and kills someone else while your grandfather is in custody."

"Oh, that's horrible!"

"Horrible, maybe, but still the truth. Two murder weapons, both your grandfather's. Two dead men, both men your grandfather had a motive to murder. Your grandfather's history as a felon. And no other suspects."

Disgusted by my lack of attention, Fancy jumped off the couch and went outside to bark at the sky. Poor girl, but she had to understand that sometimes other people took priority.

"But what about the photos? There have to be other people in there who also have a motive to kill Jack Dunner."

"Maybe. But that doesn't change the fact that the murder weapons belonged to your grandfather or that he's a felon."

"The weapons were in his truck. Anyone could've taken them from there."

"But who would know that? And who would be bold enough to come into your grandfather's driveway to take them?"

I sighed. "That's the million dollar question, isn't it? Thank you, Mr. Maxwell. I appreciate everything you've been able to do for my grandpa."

"You're welcome. I'm sorry I couldn't do more."

After I ended the call, I cooked up a grilled peanut butter and jelly sandwich—my personal version of comfort food—while I thought through my plan. Fancy, seeing that melted peanut butter was on the menu, decided to forgive me for once and for all and joined me at the table, drool spooling from her jaws as she watched me tear off a gooey bit of peanut-butter coated bread.

If only every problem were so easy to solve.

CHAPTER TWENTY-FIVE

I SPENT THE NEXT TWO HOURS PUTTING MY PLAN INTO motion, my eye on the clock as I whipped up a batch of homemade split pea soup and fresh bread from the bread maker. (I'm so glad they have that Express Bake setting, because I never think to make a loaf of bread in time to use the normal setting.) While those were cooking I gathered up everything I thought an old man might need for a night spent in jail.

It was weird to step into my grandpa's bedroom and then into his bathroom and to riffle through his things trying to figure out what he used on a daily basis. He had one of those little day-of-the-week plastic pill holders and it was still half-full, which at least saved me having to read all of his medicines and decipher which ones he was supposed to take when.

I still loaded up all the pill bottles, too, just in case someone accused me of trying to sneak recreational drugs to my eighty-two-year-old grandfather during his stint in jail. I was careful not read any of the labels, not wanting to know if he had any embarrassing prescriptions. Just my luck my grandpa would be on Viagra or something.

When the soup and bread were done, I packed them up along with some trusty little cheese sticks and all the necessities I'd put together for my grandpa and headed for the door.

Fancy had her saddest of sad faces on as she watched me leaving without her. That's what happens when you pretty much take your dog with you everywhere. When you can't take her with you, she acts like the world has ended and her heart is broken. Poor girl was having a rough day of it.

"Fine. You're getting fat, you know, but..." I ran to the kitchen and grabbed a puppy ice cream out of the freezer. "Here. I'll be back in an hour or so, okay?"

She daintily took the container from my hand and immediately went out back, her mind now on more important things. Dogs are wonderful, aren't they?

Humans, not so much.

I walked towards the police station through the chill early evening air, a large King Soopers reusable grocery bag slung over my shoulder, bumping my hip with each step. What if this didn't work? What if Matt wasn't there? What if he saw right through my ploy? And what if they wouldn't let me leave my grandpa's meds for him? Was he going to be okay until they released him?

Each step and each thump of the bag against my hip all I could think was what if, what if, what if.

But I'm good at what ifs, so for every single one I thought up, I thought of an answer too. If A then B. If C then D. On and on I thought through all the alternatives until I was as prepared as I could be.

That didn't keep away the clenching in my gut as I grasped the handle to the station door and stepped inside. The place felt even smaller at night with half the overhead lights turned off. There was a desk lamp on at Matt's desk, though, so I had hope.

He wasn't there. No one was. There'd been a soft chime as I walked in, so I was sure someone would be there soon, but I couldn't let this chance that I'd been given pass by. I carefully stepped towards Matt's desk. I knew I was taking a risk by not shouting out my presence, but if I was any judge of character—which was sorely in question these days—I knew that if I asked, Matt wouldn't let me rifle through the secrets of every person in town just to help my grandpa. I suspected that would be a line he wasn't willing to cross. Which meant I was going to have to sneak the information.

I quickly scanned the papers on his and Officer Clark's desks. There was a notepad right there in the middle of Matt's desk, covered in writing, but unfortunately it was in short hand. I'd tried to find a book or website that would let me learn it and had perused a few sites I'd found, but it still looked like gibberish to me.

Thankfully, Officer Clark did not use shorthand. There was a printed list in the center of his desk that looked very much like a high-level inventory of what they'd found in the boxes. I scanned it quickly, not sure what good it would do me. Matt was right. Pretty much everyone in town *was* on the list. It also didn't tell me *what* the folders included, just that they existed.

I took a long moment to study the list, trying to memorize what I saw, asking myself if anyone on there was a likely suspect. Four of the five people we'd thought capable of killing someone were on there, so that was one place to start.

"Found what you were looking for?" Matt asked from the hallway.

I swear, I jumped a foot at the sound of his voice. I might've squeaked loudly, too. I looked up to see him leaning against the wall, his arms crossed, like he'd been there all day.

"How long have you been there?" I asked.

"Long enough. I could arrest you for poking around a police station, you know."

I tensed for a second—I believe anything anyone says for at least one or two seconds before questioning it—but the tone of his voice said he was just teasing.

He walked towards me, slower than normal, exhaustion in every line of his body. There were dark bags under his eyes, too.

"Mason Maxwell said you're keeping my grandpa overnight." I said, more harshly than I'd planned, but there was a part of me that saw him looking so exhausted and wanted to take care of him, which was not what I needed. I was there to save my grandpa, not...I shook my head. "You said you'd try to help him."

"And I am. Why do you think I'm still here even though my shift ended two hours ago and I don't get paid for overtime?" He flung a hand at the notes on his desk. "I've looked through every single file Jack Dunner had, Maggie. None of it's worth killing over."

"To you, maybe. But for some people..." I glanced back at the list. "Like a reverend."

He rubbed at his face. "I'm just not seeing it, Maggie. But I'll look again. And I'll keep looking until I've exhausted every angle."

I nodded. It was all he could offer, after all. "I brought you and my grandpa soup. And my grandpa's medicine. He needs that, Matt. If you're going to hold an old man with a heart condition overnight, you need to let him have his pills. No point killing an innocent man."

"You know we have rules about these things…"

I didn't answer, just waited.

He sighed. "What else do you have in there?"

"Pajamas, toothbrush, toothpaste, hairbrush."

He started shaking his head as soon as the first word was out of my mouth. "The pills I'll let you leave. And, even though it's against the rules, I'll bring him out to the interrogation room for dinner—he's the only prisoner we have right now. But the rest? This is jail, Maggie, not the Ritz Carlton. The county provides all the rest of that."

I pressed my lips tight together. "Fine. Are you going to eat with us? I brought enough for three."

"You're something else, you know that?" He ran his hands through his hair. "Yeah, I'll eat with you. But no discussing the case. Agreed?"

"Agreed."

It wasn't exactly what I'd hoped for, but it was better than nothing.

I almost cried when I saw my grandpa come down the hall

in an orange jumpsuit. He looked so old and frail out of his Levi's and flannel, his shoulders slumped.

"It's going to be okay," I told him as I gave him a hard hug.

He sank into the seat Matt gestured him towards, shaking his head. "No, it's not. The damage is already done, Maggie. Poor Lesley. Why'd you tell her?"

"Because she deserved to know. Because I thought the secret was already out and that her coming forward might save you a night in jail. Or more. I was just trying to help."

He grunted as he took his first spoonful of soup, back to ignoring me. It hurt to have him angry at me, but I'd had to do what I'd done. I hadn't had another choice.

"Wow, this is really good, Maggie," Matt said, taking another bite of soup.

My grandma always said the best way to a man's heart was through his stomach, I was hoping that the best way to his mind was, too. "Thanks. So..." I started, all casual-like.

"Don't you even try to use your feminine wiles on me Miss Maggie May Carver." He tore off a hunk of bread and dunked it in his soup before taking a large enough bite to fill his mouth completely.

"Feminine wiles? What are you talking about?"

"I'm talking about you coming down here with a nice home-cooked meal and a smile and trying to get my secrets out of me. You can stop the seduction now. It's not going to work."

"Please." I opened my cheese stick. "I wouldn't know how to seduce a man if I tried. The first time I tried batting my eyes at him he'd probably ask if I had something stuck in my eye. If I'd wanted to seduce your secrets out of you, I would've sent Jamie down here instead."

My grandpa smiled slightly. "She's not trying to lie, you know. It's just that Maggie May has always underestimated the effect she has on men."

"Oh, enough. I try to do something nice by bringing both of you a real meal and this is the thanks I get? Meanwhile, poor Fancy is at home alone probably thinking she's been abandoned." I chomped into the cheese stick and glared at both of them, but neither one was the list bit rattled.

I fixed my glare on Matt. "Are you going to release my grandpa tomorrow? He doesn't deserve to be sitting in jail like this, even if you are going to charge him with murder."

"Yes. He should be out by noon. I wanted to get him processed and through today, but Officer Clark is convinced your grandpa is the worst sort of person imaginable."

"You know why, right?"

He shook his head. "No. Why?"

"I thought all small towners knew all the gossip." I glanced at my grandpa. "You knew, didn't you?"

"That his granddaddy is the one I shot? Yeah, I knew."

Matt stared at my grandpa. "The abuser you did time for killing was Ben's grandfather?"

"Yep."

"Figures. I knew there was something more there than a normal case, but I couldn't put a finger on it." He nodded to himself like a bunch of little things were suddenly clicking into place.

"So does this mean you'll let me help solve this case?" I

asked. "Tell me what you know, I'll help you brainstorm other suspects."

My grandpa snorted. "You keep helping with this case, Maggie, I'm liable to find myself in the electric chair."

"Grandpa!"

Matt shook his head. "Sorry, Maggie. I can't do it. I'd love to, but...Too many people involved now. It'd cost me my badge if I let you look through those files, and rightly so."

Ah, well. It was worth a try. And at least he'd confirmed my assessment of his character. Not that that was going to help me clear my grandpa. At least it made me confident that my grandpa really was innocent, though.

(Not that I hadn't thought he was before. But, you know, there was a lot piled up against him—not least of which was the fact that he probably *was* perfectly capable of killing a person if he saw the need for it.)

CHAPTER TWENTY-SIX

THE NEXT MORNING I WAS NO CLOSER TO FIGURING OUT who the real killer was than I'd been the night before. I'd snuck one more look at the list on Officer Clark's desk while Matt was taking my grandpa back to his cell, but without knowing what the files contained and how important each secret was to the person being blackmailed—because I assumed that's what the files were for—there was nothing there for me to work with.

Still, something about the list kept bugging me and my mind kept going back to it over and over again. There's only one thing for me to do when that happens—go for a hike. The physical movement somehow focuses my brain in a way that sitting and thinking doesn't.

So as soon as it was light enough out, I leashed up Fancy and headed for the mountain. I figured it was safe now since the cops had been all over it the day before.

I let Fancy have her way, sniffing this and that for as long as she wanted to. Part of it was guilt over how badly I'd treated her the last few days, but I'll admit I was also secretly hoping she'd find a fresh dead body that had been killed in the last twelve hours.

(Not really. I mean, okay, maybe a little? I didn't want anyone else to die, but it was the easiest way to clear my grandpa's name.)

Sadly, all she found was a dead squirrel. I made sure that's all it was before letting her do her thing since I was pretty sure the cops wouldn't be so forgiving if I let her pee on another dead body.

Eventually, we made our way up to the robber's cave, but the cops had cleared the place out. I could see from the clear space on the ground where the containers with all the blackmail information had been, but that was it. No incriminating footprints or signs that said, "The real killer is Joe Bob Smith."

So that was a bust.

I went back to my rock and sat there, looking down on the sleepy little town of Creek, counting the train cars as an early morning freight train passed through town. This one had forty-two cars, not even close to my personal record count of ninety-nine.

I could see Katie on her normal morning run, arms moving with precision, red hair swishing from side to side with each step. My grandpa said she was actually pretty good with young kids—she'd helped with the t-ball team the summer before—but I couldn't picture it. (Creek was too small for boy's teams and girl's teams, so boys and girls played together all the way until middle school when they started playing for their school teams.)

Then again, my grandpa had also said that Luke was an

excellent coach, too, so maybe he wasn't the best judge of character. I couldn't picture Luke having the patience to work with little kids. He was too much of a cad for that.

Although...Coaching was probably a prime opportunity to meet all the single moms of a certain age in town. That I could see; Luke was good with the kids because he wanted an in with the moms. Now it all made sense.

I glanced back down at Katie just in time to see her abruptly turn off the street and dash to Luke's gate. I sat forward. What the...?

She opened the gate and closed it, glancing around to make sure no one had seen her and then strode across his cluttered and cramped backyard and opened the sliding glass door.

No hesitation. Like she'd done it before.

A lot of things crashed into place in that moment. The way Luke always made sure to wink at her or kiss her cheek or flirt with her. The way she was always leaving early, usually after Luke had been by. Jamie's comment that her parents were strict and kept her on a tight leash. The flushed cheeks but no sweat when I'd seen her returning from her jog that day I'd gone down to the ballpark.

I stared intently at Luke's house, waiting for confirmation of what I now suspected—he and Katie were having an affair. That lying, no good, dirty dog. Actually, calling him a dog was an insult to all the wonderful canines of the world.

I should've known. I'd figured he'd make a move on her once she was eighteen, but before? It must've started when they were coaching together last summer...

The curtains on Luke's windows were all drawn tight so I couldn't see anything inside the house, but after about twenty minutes Luke and Katie reappeared at the sliding glass door, sharing a last passionate kiss. He didn't even have his shirt on, the creep.

I shook my head, wanting to run down that hill and pummel him into little pieces for hurting my best friend like this. Once again he'd played her for a fool. Not to mention how he was messing with Katie's head, too.

"That…"

I used a word I won't use here. And a few other words on top of that. I'd known he was a jerk. I'd known it. But I hadn't realized he was the type of guy to break the law and mess around with a seventeen-year-old girl. And he had broken the law, hadn't he?

What he was doing with Katie was illegal. There was way too much of an age difference between them for it not to be. Which meant…

Luke could be the killer.

That's what had been bugging me since I'd seen that list on Officer Clark's desk. It wasn't the names that were *on* the list, it was one of the few names that *wasn't* on the list. Lucas Dean. There should've been a folder an inch thick on him and his shenanigans, but there was nothing. Not one photo.

Because he'd killed Jack Dunner and then taken the evidence before anyone could find it.

He knew about my grandpa keeping his gun in his truck. He knew about the bat. He lived just a couple houses down from the crime scenes, so they were in his backyard, too. And he had motive.

It all fit. Lucas Dean was the killer.

I pumped my arm in the air. "I did it, Fancy. I found him."

She looked at me with one eyebrow raised, not the least bit impressed. Probably had known all along, smart girl that she was.

But I was thrilled. I could free my grandpa now. "Come on, Fancy. Let's go."

I practically dragged her down the mountainside, skipping over every root and rock in my way. It was all going to be okay now. My grandpa wasn't going to go to prison. I'd found the murderer.

CHAPTER TWENTY-SEVEN

I DROPPED FANCY OFF AT HOME, MY HANDS SHAKING IN excitement. A small part of me wanted to run straight to Luke's door and confront him with what I'd seen and what I knew. That man deserved a good what for for what'd he done to Jamie, let alone Katie and who knew who else. I bet his blackmail file was *two* inches thick.

But…

Prudence won out. If I was right, Lucas Dean had killed an old man with a baseball bat and hadn't hesitated to frame my grandpa, a man he'd worked with. Confronting someone like that was a darned good way to end up victim number three. And the only good that would come of that is they'd stop suspecting my grandpa of murder since he couldn't possibly kill me while in jail.

I decided I'd rather live through the day, thank you very much.

I headed to the police station instead, almost jogging I

was so excited. I passed right by Luke's house on the way and made a point of not looking in his direction. He'd get his soon enough and I didn't want to tip him off, not when we were so close.

Matt was already in and looked to be the only one there. I wondered if he'd ever left given the way his hair was slightly mussed and his eyes were bloodshot. He waved in my direction, but didn't move to meet me. "If you're here for your grandpa, it's going to be another hour or two before he's fully processed for release."

"No. I'm here to tell you who the real killer is." I was practically bouncing up and down.

"I've been up all night pouring over these files and you solved it? Without any evidence at all? Just thought it through, did you?"

I came around the counter and grabbed the list off of Officer Clark's desk. "Look at the list."

"I've looked at that list a hundred times, Maggie. What am I supposed to see?"

"It's not what you're supposed to see. It's what you *don't* see." I grinned at him, too excited to contain myself.

He took the list from me and looked at it once more, rubbing at his face, the scritch-scritch of his fingers rubbing against stubble the only sound in the room.

"Think about it. Who should be on that list, but isn't?" I asked.

He sighed. "I don't know. Probably a few people."

"How about Lucas Dean?"

"Luke?" He shook his head, but did scan the list to confirm his name wasn't there. He set the list down and leaned against the desk, arms crossed. "I've known Luke since we were kids. He doesn't have it in him to kill someone."

I pressed my lips together, deflating like a popped balloon. He was supposed to believe me, not question me like this. "You know him so well, do you?"

"Maggie..."

"Do you think he has it in him to take up with a seventeen-year-old girl?"

Matt opened his mouth and then shut it again. He frowned. "Katie?"

"Yep. I just saw them together. I was up the mountain behind his house and saw her sneak in through his backyard. They came back maybe twenty minutes later, shared a passionate kiss—him without his shirt on—and then she left."

He grunted.

"Did you see that in him?" I asked.

He shrugged one shoulder. "No. But I can see that before I can see murder."

"But don't you get it? If Jack Dunner found out about him and Katie and tried to blackmail him...Maybe Luke decided it was safer to just eliminate Dunner rather than pay him."

"And Roy Jackson?"

"Maybe he saw them together, too. He was certainly on that path often enough. I know there was the one morning when I took Fancy out for a walk that I saw Katie running—towards Luke's house, obviously—around the same time I saw Mr. Jackson headed up the mountain. If he saw what Luke was doing and confronted him about it..."

Matt thought about it for a long moment.

I wanted to grab him and shake him. It was so obvious. Finally, he pushed off of the desk. "You're right. It all does fit. I'll bring him in."

I whooped and Matt leveled a steady stare at me. "He may not be the killer, Maggie. I'll grant you he's the best alternate suspect we've had so far, but it might not be him."

I waved his concern away. I knew it was Luke. I knew it. It all fit together perfectly. And Matt would see it, too. He just needed a little time, that's all.

Luke was going to be arrested for murder. Today. Which meant I needed to go see Jamie. She deserved to hear about this from me instead of from some gossipy busybody who happened to visit the café after word got out.

"So you're going to bring him in?" I confirmed.

"Yes. As soon as Marlene arrives, I'll go get him." He glanced at the clock on the wall. "Should be about fifteen minutes from now."

I flashed him a smile. "Thank you," I shouted as I ran out the door.

Finally, everything was falling into place.

I was so excited, I ran the whole way back to my grandpa's place. Not the best of ideas since I never run. I had to stop on the front porch and gasp for breath as I held my side against the sharp pain I felt there. I could've sworn I'd developed shin splints, too, but I was pretty sure that was just my middle-aged body being overly dramatic.

Fancy cried at me through the doorway until I let myself

inside. As I waited for Matt to arrest Luke, I debated calling Jamie to tell her what had happened, but I knew this was the kind of news that was best delivered in person. I quickly changed instead, so I'd be ready to go as soon as it happened.

When eight o'clock rolled around I stationed myself at the kitchen window and watched for any sign of Matt or Luke. A few minutes later I saw Matt walk out of the police station—at least it looked like him, I was just far enough away to not be positive. Whoever it was walked down the street to Luke's house and disappeared from view.

I braced myself, wondering just how dangerous Luke was. What if he tried to run? What if he pulled a gun on Matt? Or a baseball bat?

But, no. I could see him killing when trapped in a corner like he had with Jack Dunner, but killing someone he'd known since he could walk? Nah. Lucas Dean was bad, but he wasn't that bad.

And I was right. Because a few minutes later I saw two men leave Luke's house and walk towards the police station, chatting casually. The one that must be Luke had his hands in his pockets, completely at ease as he walked next to the officer.

Honestly, I think Matt should've hauled Luke in in cuffs for the Katie thing, but I was starting to realize that just wasn't his style. It must be hard to be a cop in a small town where you know everyone. You aren't just arresting a perp, you're arresting someone you played football with or whose dad coached you in baseball. I had to feel for the guy. But not too much. Not if that got in the way of him finding the real killer.

I waited until they made it back to the station and then leashed up Fancy and headed for the barkery.

CHAPTER TWENTY-EIGHT

THE WHOLE DRIVE I WAS FIDGETY, GOING OVER THINGS again and again and again. It had to be Luke. It had to be. It made so much sense. There was no blackmail file on him. He knew about the bat and the gun. He lived right there. He had a secret to hide. And it was a big enough one that people would kill for it.

But...

He was Luke. Worthless cad and flirt who'd probably sleep with anyone he could, but was he really a killer? Would he really take a *baseball bat* to someone?

Eh.

Maybe?

But if it wasn't Luke then I was back at square one and my grandpa was back to being the one and only real suspect.

I so wanted it to be Luke, but the closer I got to the barkery the more I wondered if it really was. I still needed to tell Jamie about Luke and Katie, because he was going to go to jail for that...Maybe. Except the pictures were gone if they'd ever existed. And I was the only one who'd seen them together. And all I'd seen was them kissing, which I was pretty sure was not illegal.

I felt nauseous thinking that Luke might get away with that. Especially knowing Jamie and her never-ending ability to forgive people for their flaws. It wasn't that I didn't have flaws of my own—I had plenty—it was just that I didn't see the point of letting anyone off the hook for it. If you were mean, you should admit you were mean. If you used others, you should admit that, too. And you should be told it was wrong and to try better next time. Not forgiven every frickin' time.

Of course, one of the reasons Jamie and I were such good friends was that very capacity of hers to forgive people when they messed up and to not hold a grudge. See, I could be friends with Jamie because she was just a genuinely good person who didn't hurt others. She could be friends with me because she forgave and forgot when I was prickly and rude.

I pulled up outside the store, all of my earlier excitement gone. Sure, it was possible Luke was still the killer, but Matt's words had wiggled their way into my brain and made me doubt it. And I just knew in my gut of guts that Luke was going to get a pass for the Katie thing. Because what love-struck seventeen-year-old is willing to turn on her older boyfriend? None.

Ugh.

As usual, Fancy didn't let me sit and brood, barking her head off and demanding to be let out of the van as soon as we were parked. She dragged me right for the entrance, too, probably eager to see Lulu. Jamie didn't bring Lulu in every single day the way I did Fancy, but she'd started bringing her in more and more.

Fancy and Lulu were double trouble. They adored each other, but had their moments of insanity, too. Puppy teeth are sharp and Fancy's paw of doom was not to be underestimated. I let Fancy drag me towards the door, trying to figure out what I was going to say to Jamie.

Should I tell her anything at all?

The breakfast rush had just about ended. Katie was wiping down the tables and taking dishes to the kitchen while Jamie rang up the last customer. I glanced towards the barkery side, trying not to feel sad at how quiet it looked. At least online sales were ticking along nicely...

As soon as the last customer left—a man I didn't recognize who had the definite look of a tourist with his fancy sunglasses—I let Fancy off her leash. She immediately ran to the cubby where Lulu had been sleeping and the two proceeded to cry and lick and bite at each other.

I almost laughed at the way Fancy's tail swished back and forth, but instead I turned my attention to Jamie. And Katie; I'd forgotten she'd be there.

Jamie tilted her head to the side. "Hey, Mags. I thought I told you to stay at home today. How's your grandpa?"

"They should be releasing him in an hour or so. At least Matt, Officer Barnes, let me bring him his meds last night. Who knows what shape he'd be in otherwise."

"So they really think he did it, huh? Your grandpa? That just doesn't fit, does it?"

Katie walked back out of the kitchen. "Yes, it does. That man is definitely capable of killing someone."

I blinked slowly, stunned by her words. My grandpa actually liked her. I couldn't believe she'd just said that about him. I mean, granted, I'd thought it a time or two myself. And it was probably true, but…Who says that kind of thing?

"He didn't kill anyone," I said, lashing out. "It was Lucas Dean."

Katie dropped the plate she'd been holding and it shattered on the floor just as I realized what I'd said. "Jamie…"

I stepped toward her.

"What are you talking about?" she asked, her hands shaking as she tried to figure out what to do with them. "Luke? He's not a killer? Why would he…? It can't be Luke."

"It wasn't Luke." Katie was there next to me, her eyes flashing with anger—the first time I'd seen real emotion from her. She'd picked up a piece of the shattered plate and it must've cut her because blood was dripping from her hand onto the floor.

"It wasn't Luke!" she screeched.

I stepped back from her, finally seeing what I'd missed. She was right. It wasn't Luke. It was her. It was Katie.

Katie had known about the gun. And the bat. She'd been there when I told Jamie about my grandpa threatening Jack Dunner and about the robber's cave. She had the same secret to hide. It wouldn't put her in jail, but if she was in love with Luke…

"You're right. It wasn't Luke, was it, Katie?" I took another step back.

Jamie was frozen behind the counter.

"It was you, wasn't it, Katie?" I asked. "Why did you do it? Why did you kill those two men?"

She tightened her grip on the broken plate and it sliced deeper into her palm, blood flowing in a steady stream to the floor. Part of me wanted to take the plate away from her before she hurt herself worse, but another part of me was sort of hoping she'd lose enough blood to faint because I wasn't too interested in fighting a teenaged murderess who'd already killed two people.

Jamie started to come around the counter, but I waved her back. "Stay back, Jamie. She's dangerous. She killed Jack Dunner and Mr. Jackson."

"Did you? Katie? Why?"

Katie wasn't looking at anything we could see, but she nodded slowly. "I was going to lose Luke…He said we had to stop…"

She shook her head, like she was trying to clear it of something.

I slowly reached for the cellphone in the outer pocket of my purse, hoping she wouldn't see it, but she dropped the plate and grabbed a steak knife off a nearby table, lunging at me with it, her eyes wild. "Don't. Put it away. Over there." She gestured towards the corner.

I threw the phone away from me, risking a glance towards Jamie who'd started inching her way towards the store phone. All she had to do was get it off the hook and dial 9-1-1. That's all she had to do. But as she took a step towards the phone, Katie screeched at her and sliced her knife through the air.

"And you!" She swiped at Jamie again. "You were going to take him from me. He loved *me* until *you* showed up." She swiped at Jamie again and I started to back towards where I'd tossed my phone, but Fancy chose that moment to notice what was going on and came running, barking her head off.

I lunged for her collar and pulled her back just as Katie swept her knife towards Fancy. That awoke a fury in me that I could barely contain. "What is wrong with you," I screamed at her.

I know—this girl had already killed two people and was looking like she was going to try to kill me or Jamie, too, but I didn't lose it until she threatened my dog. What can I say? I have some very skewed priorities. Plus, Jamie and I could handle ourselves. Fancy...

Well, it turned out Fancy could handle herself, too.

She tore free of my grip and ran right at Katie, snarling. I'd never seen her do that before, but let me tell you that when a hundred-and-forty-pound dog comes at you, teeth bared, it can be downright scary. Scary enough that Katie shrieked, dropped her knife, and ran towards the corner of the store.

Fancy cornered her there, barking her head off in her "you've really upset me and I want you to know it" bark. I raced to my cellphone and hit Emergency, but hung up a moment later.

Because pulling into the parking lot outside was Officer Matthew Allen Barnes. My white knight—if he'd been about five minutes earlier, and hadn't had Lucas Dean with him, seated in the passenger seat instead of cuffed in the back like he deserved.

CHAPTER TWENTY-NINE

"FANCY. ENOUGH," I SAID, CUTTING THROUGH HER barking, as Matt and Luke came inside. She glanced back at me, clearly not ready to let it go, but when she saw Matt she wagged her tail and ran over to him. Traitor.

Luke stepped past Matt and Fancy and headed for Katie.

"Luke? What are you doing here?" she asked, her voice trembling as she swayed on her feet, her hand still dripping blood all over the floor.

I almost felt sorry for her then. Almost.

"Katie, what have you done?" He stepped closer, hands held up to calm her.

"I just wanted us to be together..." she whispered. "I just...We were going to go to Mexico when I turned eighteen. Remember? I..." She started weeping. "I just wanted us to be together. I just wanted us to be together."

"Oh, Katie." He pulled her close as she sobbed into his shoulder. "I'm so sorry."

I glanced at Jamie. She was watching them with a frown, her arms crossed. I realized she still didn't know about Luke and Katie. I stepped closer. "I saw them together this morning. At Luke's house. I thought that meant Luke was the murderer. I came here to tell you."

Jamie looked at me, dazed. "But...He and I..."

I shrugged, not wanting to remind her in that moment that Luke was a cheaty cheat cheater and was never going to change.

Fancy finally ambled over to my side and I put her back on her leash. The store was a mess, blood all over the floor, tracked there by her giant paws, but I didn't care. I was just glad to have her back by my side.

I heard sirens and glanced up to see an ambulance pulling up outside. I guess Katie did need it, although honestly I was okay with her bleeding out a little bit more first. (She'd threatened my dog and my best friend. You don't do that and expect me to care one whit about you.)

Matt saw my look and gave me a half grin and shake of the head as another officer arrived. He turned to brief him, pointing towards Katie and then the ambulance. The officer went over to Luke and Katie and they slowly walked out to the ambulance as Matt came over to join me and Jamie.

"I told you it wasn't Luke." He leaned against the counter like he owned it.

I gave him my death stare, but it didn't faze him one bit. He glanced at the bloody floor. "What exactly happened here?"

I met his unflappable look with one of my own. "Katie didn't like it either when I said Luke was the killer. That's when I realized who the killer really was. She grabbed a knife and I think would've hurt one of us, but then Fancy came to the rescue."

I scratched at Fancy's ears. "Who knew you had it in you, girl?"

She just groaned and leaned into my hand, all signs of her ferocious snarl long gone.

"So Fancy's the hero of the day, is she?" Matt walked over to the barkery side and grabbed a Doggie Delight out of the case. "I think your mother would agree that you've earned a special treat, young lady."

Fancy sat, waiting for him to give it to her, patient as patient could be, drool forming a puddle at her feet, but Lulu started barking up a storm, not wanting to be left out if treats were on offer.

I shook my head and grabbed her one, too. Dogs. Gotta love 'em.

CHAPTER THIRTY

I SHOOED BOTH OF THE DOGS OUT BACK INTO THE DOG
run, figuring we had enough bloody paw prints already, we
didn't need to add to the count. When I came back inside
Matt and Jamie were talking quietly, leaning close to one
another across the counter. For a brief moment I felt almost
jealous, but then I remembered that I was the one who'd
told Jamie to go for him. I reminded myself that if Jamie
ended up with a guy like Matt that would be the best thing
in the world.

Far better than her ending up with Luke. I let them have
a moment and then joined them. "Are you going to charge
him?" I asked. "For the Katie thing?"

Matt winced. "I don't know. That'll depend on what
Katie says. We have no photos, remember?"

I glanced at Jamie, not wanting to hurt her, but not
wanting to see Lucas Dean get off scot-free for what had
happened. "I know what I saw. They were...together."

Jamie grabbed a rag from the bleach bucket under the

counter and started scrubbing at the blood stains. "Nobody's perfect, Maggie."

I didn't want to argue with her. Not today. Not when so much ugliness had already happened. She'd come around eventually, once she really thought about what he'd done, she just needed time to see it.

Instead I turned back to Matt. "By the way, you better make sure to charge Katie with two counts of murder and one count of attempted murder."

"For what happened here, today? Wouldn't that be two counts of attempted murder? And it's not like she really wanted to kill you guys, she was just upset that her whole world was unraveling."

"No. Not for today." I glanced at Jamie. "For the explosion. In the kitchen. I'm pretty sure that was Katie's fault, too. It was just her and Jamie here that day and she was conveniently outside when it happened."

Jamie turned back to me, mouth hanging open. "Do you really think…?"

I nodded. "Yeah. I do. I think she was crazy in love with Luke and that when you showed up and he started showing you attention that she wanted you gone so she could have him all to herself again. Jealousy of you was probably what made her snap in the first place. Jack Dunner and Mr. Jackson happened after that."

Jamie sank into a chair and buried her face in her hands. "How did I not see it?"

Matt squeezed my hand before stepping back. "How about I get your statements later."

"Thanks. Appreciate it."

I locked the door after him, flipped the café sign to

closed, and grabbed us two beers from the mini fridge. "Come on, Jamie. Let's go outside with the pups."

She glanced at the beers in my hand. "It's not even noon, Maggie."

"Eh. It's five o'clock somewhere. And if the last hour didn't make you want to have a drink, I don't know what would. Now come on. Let's go."

We spent the next hour sitting outside on a gorgeous early summer day, the wind blowing through the trees, trying to make sense of the last few weeks as our dogs slept in the shade nearby. Neither one of us wanted to deal with the mess inside, although we knew we'd have to eventually.

For the time being it was just enough to know that we were both safe and that my grandpa was going to be freed. Jamie still couldn't wrap her mind around the whole Luke and Katie thing—any of it—and I sort of doubted she ever would. She's one of those rare people who sees the good in everyone, even the murderers, liars, and cheats. Part of me was glad this hadn't ruined her. Part of me wished she'd wisen up a bit, especially if Luke didn't end up spending at least six months in jail for his little affair with Katie.

I did at least manage to convince her to let me ban him from the store for life. It wasn't much, but it was progress.

As I sat there drinking a beer with my best friend way too early in the morning, I took a deep breath.

My move to Creek hadn't turned out at all the way I'd thought it would. My grandpa wasn't the feeble, needy old man I'd believed him to be, but was instead spry, stubborn, and, most surprising of all, in love. The valley wasn't the haven from the real world I'd always imagined, either. I knew now that people there were full of the same wants and needs, hatreds and loves as anywhere else.

The barkery wasn't yet the raging success I'd hoped for. There was an annoyingly handsome cop I couldn't stop thinking about. We were down one shop assistant. Our store was covered in blood. Jamie was probably still in love with Luke…

Despite all that, it was still the best decision I'd ever made to move to the valley. I was glad that my grandpa was probably going to be around a lot longer than I'd thought. And that I lived somewhere with people as real and flawed as I was.

And I was still living in one of the most gorgeous places in the world, running a business I loved, with my best friend in the world and Miss Fancypants at my side. Life wasn't perfect, but I couldn't imagine it being much better.

If I could just get through the next month without someone else being murdered, life would be very good indeed.

ABOUT THE AUTHOR

When Aleksa Baxter decided to write what she loves it was a no-brainer to write a cozy mystery set in the mountains of Colorado where she grew up and starring a Newfie, Miss Fancypants, that is very much like her own Newfie, in both the good ways and the bad.

You can reach her at aleksabaxterwriter@gmail.com or on her website aleksabaxter.com.

To hear about new releases or promotions, sign up for her mailing list.

Made in the USA
San Bernardino, CA
13 December 2018